'Ahhh!'

Patricia stopped dead in her tracks, unable to stifle the groan forced on her by a searing pain. Yes, this was definitely it!

As she doubled up in anguish she became aware that someone sitting in one of the cars was getting out. Oh, bliss! Like a mirage in the desert, Adam Young, her wonderful new friend, was sprinting towards her!

Margaret Barker pursued a variety of interesting careers before she became a full-time author. Besides holding a BA degree in French and Linguistics, she is a Licentiate of the Royal Academy of Music, a State Registered Nurse and a qualified teacher. Happily married, she has two sons, a daughter, and an increasing number of grandchildren. She lives with her husband in a sixteenth-century thatched house near the East Anglian coast.

Recent titles by the same author:

RELUCTANT PARTNERS

THE PREGNANT DOCTOR

BY
MARGARET BARKER

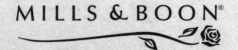

MILLS & BOON®

*First published in Great Britain 2001
Harlequin Mills & Boon Limited,
Eton House, 18-24 Paradise Road, Richmond, Surrey TW9 1SR*

© Margaret Barker 2001

ISBN 0 263 82677 5

*Set in Times Roman 10½ on 12 pt.
03-0701-50041*

*Printed and bound in Spain
by Litografía Rosés, S.A., Barcelona*

CHAPTER ONE

PATRICIA was trying desperately to pull the edges of her coat over her bump. When she'd first bought this voluminous garment at the beginning of her pregnancy she'd never imagined she would actually fill it. She remembered how the shop assistant in Mothercare, a kindly motherly sort who'd been only too happy to talk about her own children and grandchildren, had been adamant that she would be the size of a house before she'd produced her baby.

She'd been absolutely right! Patricia hadn't told the mature, helpful lady that she was a doctor and had cared for lots of pregnant patients and delivered many babies. Somehow, being pregnant yourself changed the whole scenario, made you feel terribly vulnerable. And all the medical theory and experience she'd acquired since she'd begun medical school at the age of eighteen until now, when she'd arrived at the vast age of thirty-one, hadn't prepared her for feeling like a beached whale.

She wriggled on the small wooden chair trying to make herself more comfortable as she looked around the surgery waiting room.

'Welcome to Highdale Practice,' said the noticeboard. 'Here are some of the medical facilities we would like to offer you.'

Patricia leaned back against the hard, uncomfortable chair. Just offer me this job—that's all I ask! It seemed so strange to be coming for an interview when she was thirty-eight weeks pregnant. How lucky she was that this

GP appointment wouldn't require her to start work until next April. If she had the baby on schedule in two weeks' time, that would mean it would be nearly six months old by the time she started work.

She gave an involuntary sigh as she reprimanded herself for thinking that she'd got the job already.

'Are you OK?'

She turned to look at the person sitting next to her, who'd just spoken, and smiled.

'I'm fine, thanks.'

What a dishy man! She'd been so concerned with trying to shrink anonymously into her chair that she hadn't noticed him. Wonderfully warm brown eyes, devastatingly handsome face and those long legs stretched out in front of him would carry him heavenwards, way beyond her reach.

Way beyond her reach in every sense! But she wouldn't have minded meeting someone like this in her pre-responsibility days. Even though she was small in stature herself, she would find it fun to stand on tiptoe and gaze up into those expressive eyes.

Fun! That was something she hadn't experienced for a few months, not since she'd broken off her engagement to that rat of a man who'd two-timed her. Patricia squirmed in her seat as the memories of Ben's duplicity flooded back. That awful day when she'd woken up in blissful ignorance and had then actually discovered him—

'Are you sure you wouldn't like me to get you something? A drink of water perhaps? You look so…uncomfortable.'

That velvety, deeply soothing voice again. He would have one hell of a bedside manner, this doctor! She presumed he must be a doctor otherwise he wouldn't be sitting here with the two other candidates beside herself, waiting for a final interview.

She smiled again at her fellow candidate, remembering that Ben had always said her delicate elfin face was one of her best features. Well, her face hadn't changed, even though the rest of her resembled a hot-air balloon. And the Leeds hairdressing salon had made a good job of sorting out her short blonde hair yesterday in readiness for the next few months when she wouldn't have much time to herself.

At the thought of the impending weeks Patricia felt a pang of apprehension. She was longing to have this baby. She loved it so much already—it didn't have a sex yet because the scans hadn't been conclusive—so she just knew she was going to be one of these doting mothers who bored their childless colleagues with stories of her child's exploits. But the thought of the actual birth wasn't something she liked to dwell on…

She realised that the stranger was still looking concerned as he waited for her to reply.

'That's very kind of you, but I'm OK, really,' she said quickly. 'I'll be fine when this interview is over.'

'Won't we all?' He smiled back, revealing the most wonderfully even white teeth.

Patricia uncurled her fingers from the edges of her coat, allowing it to fall to the sides of her bump. She was going to be proud of her baby when it was born so why should she cover it up now?

She grinned. 'I hate interviews at the best of times, and now's not exactly an ideal time for me.'

'I think you're very brave,' he told her in that soothing voice that made her feel good about herself.

'No alternative. Jane and Richard told me they wanted to get the new appointments finalised before April.'

'So, do you know Jane and Richard?' Dr Dishy
Brown Eyes asked her.

She hesitated, hoping he wasn't insinuating that it was
preferential treatment that had got her on the final short
list.

'I was at medical school at Moortown General with
them. Jane was in my year and Richard was a few years
older.' She paused. 'Don't worry—they're not the kind
of people who dish out favours on the old boy and girl
network. They'll appoint whoever's best for the job.
Anyway, I'm applying for the part-time job-share with
Jane, not the full-time appointment, so—'

'Dr Adam Young,' the receptionist called from her
desk near the door. 'Would you like to go in now?'

Her new friend stood up and as Patricia had surmised
he was incredibly tall! As he looked down at her from
his great height, his dark brown hair flopped over his
forehead and for the first time in months she experienced
a shiver of serious attraction running through her.

'Good luck!'

'Thanks!'

She felt a sense of loss as he disappeared through the
door. It occurred to her that she could start up a conversation with the severe-looking woman sitting directly
opposite, but Patricia had already noticed her wedding
ring and was wondering if she was the opposition.
Probably. It was usually married women with family
commitments who applied for part-time jobs. Anyway,
this woman was making it perfectly obvious she didn't
want to talk as she sorted out papers from her important-
looking, executive-type leather briefcase.

The man in the corner with the deadly serious expression was talking into his mobile again. What a bore!
His loud, abrasive voice was very intrusive as he read-

ranged his busy schedule with some unseen colleague. He was probably Adam Young's rival for the full-time appointment. If she got the job here she knew who she'd prefer to be working with!

Patricia rubbed her hands down the side of her back, which had been aching on and off all day. As she'd often told her obstetric patients, this was one of the discomforts in the later stages of pregnancy. The ligaments in her body had relaxed to allow the baby to grow, and unless she took great care with her posture and took adequate rest she would just have to put up with it. It was only two weeks since she'd finished working as a full-time GP in Leeds and these last few days had been hectic. She knew perfectly well that she'd been working too hard.

She consoled herself with the thought that these final interviews were only a few minutes each, not like the lengthy session she'd had a couple of months ago. So it wouldn't be long before she'd be home and propped up on the sofa with a nice cup of tea in time to watch the early evening news. And then she really would take care of herself for the last two weeks.

Patricia tensed as the backache grew stronger. How strong was strong? She'd often thought there should be some kind of scale, like scientists had when they measured earthquakes, for the general non-specific backache that plagued many of her patients. When someone came to the surgery and told her they had terrible backache she tended to gauge it by who the patient was and what their own personal pain threshold seemed to be before she started on the appropriate tests.

She picked up a magazine from the table beside her and flicked through it. There was an article called 'Happy Families' about how it was important to include your partner in sharing every aspect of your pregnancy, the highs and the lows. And when the baby was born your partner should experience the joy and help you through the pain. Patricia swallowed hard. Quite right! Very sound advice…only she'd been on her own since the conception and would be very much on her own at the birth.

She scrabbled for a tissue at the bottom of her bag and blew her nose. It was no good feeling sorry for herself. It had been her own choice to break off the engagement. Ben had wanted everything to carry on where they'd left off, but nobody treated her in such a humiliating way and got away with it!

The door was opening. He was coming out, this handsome man who'd brightened up her day. She felt her spirits lifting as she turned to smile at him.

'How did it go?'

He gave her a wry grin. 'Difficult to tell. They're going to let me know, so I'll just have to remain in suspense until I get that all-important phone call.'

'Dr Patricia Drayton. Would you like to go in now?' said the receptionist.

She began to heave herself up. Adam Young moved swiftly forward and held out both hands. Gratefully she took them and felt the strength of him lifting her. For an instant she felt as light as a feather and almost attractive—but not quite! The reality of her cover-up coat and voluminous wrap-around skirt soon brought her back to earth.

'Thanks,' Patricia said quietly.

'Good luck,' he whispered.

As she moved towards the consulting-room door, one hand on the section of her back that was causing her the most pain at the moment, she felt a pang of sadness that her new friend was leaving before she'd had time to get to know him.

Jane and Richard were at their most helpful in trying to put her at her ease, but the discomfort she was feeling was making her tense as she answered the first few questions.

'Are you feeling all right, Patricia?' Jane asked.

'I'm fine. Just a little discomfort, that's all, but that will clear in a couple of weeks.'

'And you'll be fighting fit by next April,' Richard said. 'That's all that we're concerned about today. As you know, the population in this area is expanding rapidly due to the new housing estate that's being built for the convenience of commuters to Leeds and Moortown and the holiday complex that's going up down by the river. Jane and I can cope with the patients we've got at the moment, but by next April it's going to be another story.'

'Yes, we know your record of achievement as a successful GP in Leeds,' Jane said. 'You may feel a bit vulnerable now in your late stage of pregnancy but we know what you're really like.'

'Now, have you sorted out the arrangements you could make for next April, should you be appointed?' Richard asked. 'We need to know that you would be able to cope with your baby and share Jane's workload. With a four-month-old baby ourselves we know the problems you might have.'

He flashed a brief glance at his wife who returned his look with adoring eyes. Patricia could see these two were still madly in love. She remembered how thrilled she'd been to be invited to their wedding last Christmas. Jane had confided that she was three months pregnant and that she and Richard were over the moon about it. They had kept it secret from all but a few close friends until a general announcement about the happy situation had been necessary.

She'd felt privileged to be among the few close friends chosen to share in the secret. But she remembered how she and Jane had always shared secrets when they'd been at medical school together. They'd been very close.

But that wasn't going to help her get this job if she didn't convince them she had more to offer than the other candidate on the short-list! And she must also make it quite clear that she'd made adequate arrangements for the care of her baby.

'I'm planning to rent a small house in Highdale if I'm appointed, and my sister, who has two children, has agreed to look after the baby when I'm on duty.'

Jane smiled. 'Well, that seems to sort out the domestic situation in a satisfactory way.'

She glanced enquiringly at her husband who still seemed intent on asking more questions.

'What made you want to leave the practice in Leeds?'

'I've always known I would prefer to work in a country practice. As you know, my roots are here in Highdale where I've still got family. And the practice in Leeds was where I trained as a GP. It's best to move on if you can after a few years. You're always regarded as the novice until you do.'

Jane nodded in agreement. 'Very true. My father still thinks I'm playing at doctors, even though, theoretically, I'm the senior partner here.'

Patricia warmed once again to her friend. 'As you know, I did apply for the appointment when your father retired nineteen months ago, but Richard pipped me at the post.'

Richard's serious expression relaxed and he smiled. 'I think you would have got it if Jane hadn't been overruled by her father. He pointed out that you were planning to be married and move to London in a couple of years so Jane agreed, reluctantly I might add, to take me on.'

Jane smiled affectionately. 'And look where that got me!'

Richard laughed, then, as if remembering he was supposed to be conducting an interview, he adopted his serious expression again.

Patricia relaxed against the back of her chair. It was so strange to be sitting here with these two dear friends, trying to be professional. The first interview had been much more serious and she'd been almost overawed by their utter dedication to the job of appointing the person who would best serve the practice. But today the strain of keeping up the unnatural situation of interviewers and interviewee was beginning to show.

Looking at them now, she could see that marriage suited them perfectly. Jane had been rather plain in her early years, but now she was glowing with health and inner beauty. Her once mousy coloured hair was beautifully cut and streaked with blonde highlights. Richard was still as classically tall, dark and handsome as he'd always been. Now in his late thirties, he'd retained the athletic figure that had turned heads at medical school and had had the girls vying for his attention.

She knew he was a good doctor and so was Jane. Oh, it would be so great to work with them! Patricia stifled a groan as she felt the backache impinging deeper inside her. This time it wasn't just her back that felt the pain.

Oh, no! It couldn't be! Not two weeks before she was due.

She took a deep breath, knowing that it might well be an early labour. But there would be plenty of time even if it were. First babies were notoriously slow to arrive. There was definitely time to get through this final interview without causing problems. She wanted a fair interview with no favours granted for friendship, so she would make sure Jane and Richard didn't know she was beginning to get worried.

'We were really sorry to hear the wedding was off,' Richard said in a sympathetic tone.

'Most definitely off!'

'No chance of a reconciliation?' he asked quietly.

'None whatsoever! I firmly believe that marriage should be founded on mutual trust, and if that trust is broken by one of the partners, there's no point in going on with the relationship.'

'You seem to have come to terms with the situation very well,' Jane said in a soothing tone. 'Well, now, just a few more questions about the differences you would experience working up here in the Dales compared to the city...'

Somehow, Patricia managed to concentrate on her answers in a coherent, professional manner. Minutes later, she was free to go.

Richard stood up and grasped her hand as she struggled to her feet. 'We'll give you a call, Patricia, as soon as we've made up our minds. Don't worry, we won't keep you in suspense very long. Take care of yourself.'

He moved to hold open the door and she waddled outside. She breathed a sigh of relief as the door closed behind her. She'd felt very confident after the first interview but today she didn't know how she felt. Muddled, desperate to escape and put her feet up, longing for this pain to stop nagging her.

Fresh air, that was what she needed! She made for the outer door as quickly as was humanly possible, considering that her enormous bulk was impeding her progress. She could see her car in the car park. She began to make her way towards it, getting slower with every step.

'Ah-h-h!' Patricia stopped dead in her tracks, unable to stifle the groan forced on her by a searing pain. Yes, this was definitely it!

As she doubled up in anguish she became aware that someone sitting in one of the cars was getting out. Oh, bliss! Like a mirage in the desert, Adam Young, her wonderful new friend, was sprinting towards her! She could feel she was in danger of collapsing but he was now telling her to lean on him. Gratefully, she took him at his word, hoping that he wouldn't crumple under her enormous weight.

He was leading her towards his small, sleek, black car, opening the passenger door for her. Patricia hadn't the strength to argue as she sank down onto the seat and looked up into his eyes. His concerned expression made her feel almost human again.

'Tell me how you're really feeling,' he said firmly. 'And stop trying to disguise your symptoms.'

She took a deep breath. 'I'm only thirty-eight weeks pregnant but I think I'm going into labour, so I'll just sit here for a moment to gather my strength and then I'll get in my own car, drive down to Moortown General and—'

'You'll do nothing of the sort. It's not safe for you to drive in your condition. I'll drive you.'

'I could phone for an ambulance.'

Dr Young shook his head. 'It will be quicker if I take you. I don't want you hanging around here any longer than necessary.'

Oh, the joy of being with someone who appeared as if he really cared! She'd known he would have a good bedside manner.

'Are you sure there's no one you'd like me to call?' he said carefully.

'I'm on my own,' Patricia said quickly. 'It's…' She hesitated. 'It's just how things have turned out.'

He was climbing into the driver's seat. 'Well, if you're sure.' The engine sprang to life.

'It's a good thing I was still here in the car park. I've got some time to kill before I need to be back at the airport so I was taking a rest before driving around to have a look at the surrounding countryside. This is only a hire car but it seems reliable. I've taken it for a few days while I'm over here from the States. I'd have got something bigger if I'd known I was going to have to carry someone in your condition.'

Patricia managed a weak smile. 'Are you suggesting I'm too big for normal transport?'

She watched his handsome face crease into a grin. 'Won't be long now before you're slim again. In my medical experience you tiny girls balloon out enormously because the baby and its baggage fills up so much space in the abdomen. But once you've delivered you shed the weight quicker than the tall girls who've stashed away pockets of fat in their larger frames.'

'Not necessarily. I've known— Ah-h-h!' Patricia put both hands over her abdomen as the searing pain began again. Automatically, she began to pant. 'I think I'm…'

Adam Young put his foot down harder on the accelerator. 'I think you are, too, but I'll get you to the hospital as quickly as I can. And even if we don't make it in time it won't be the first baby I've delivered in a strange situation.'

The situation couldn't have been stranger, she thought as they hurtled along the country lanes. Hedgerows, limestone walls, a stray sheep that objected to having to hurry across the road, tall overhanging trees shedding their autumnal leaves—everything seemed to fly past her in a blur. This was a definite contraction she was experiencing now! She'd better regularise her panting technique because it didn't seem to be doing anything to ease the pain.

Instinctively, she reached out to grab hold of the nearest person who could offer her support. Squeezing Adam's arm reassured her that she wasn't alone. As the contraction diminished Patricia flopped against him across the gear shift in the middle of the car.

'Good thing this is an automatic car,' she said as she snuggled against him for comfort. 'You wouldn't be able to change gear with me gumming up the works.'

'Are you sure you don't want me to pull in and check how things are going?'

'Let's just get to the hospital,' she said quickly. The thought of a roadside delivery was distinctly unappealing!

Adam took one hand off the wheel and squeezed hers. 'You're a real trouper! Hang on in there!'

She gave a weak laugh. 'Got no choice, have I? Ah-h-h…!'

As the contraction grew in intensity she pulled his hand to her face, pressing it against her mouth so that she wouldn't cry out again. She breathed in the faint aroma of some masculine-type soap and took comfort in the fact that he was making gentle sounds of encouragement, little oohs and ahs of sympathy.

'Nearly there, Patricia.'

She clung to his hand, pushing it up to her damp forehead so that his natural reaction was to gently stroke her. She leaned more heavily against this wonderful source of comfort. 'Ah, that's nice,' she whispered as he stroked her hair back from her forehead.

Suddenly his soothing hand was back on the wheel as he negotiated the corner into the hospital forecourt. Patricia began to pant as another contraction claimed all her attention. She was vaguely aware that she was being lifted onto a trolley. She reached up and grabbed Adam's hand.

'Don't leave me, will you?' she said in a panic-stricken voice.

'Of course I won't,' he said soothingly, as he squeezed her hand.

She closed her eyes, secure in the knowledge that her knight in shining armour was still beside her and would be with her throughout the ordeal that was to come. For a brief moment between contractions Patricia remembered how positive she'd always been with her patients, even the ones with obstetric complications. She'd assured them that there was nothing to worry about, that they were in safe hands.

She tried to convince herself that was the case now. Nothing could go wrong, could it? None of the complications she'd witnessed when she'd been doing her obstetrics training in this very hospital, in the obstetrics unit where they were taking her now...

Patricia opened her eyes and felt safe again as she saw Adam looking down at her with that comfortingly concerned expression.

'You're going to be fine,' he told her gently, as if he understood what was going through her head. 'You're in an excellent hospital with first-class staff. As you well know, the majority of births are perfectly normal. You and I have seen the exceptions, but with modern technology there's always a way of dealing with those exceptions.'

She was going through swing doors. Bright lights were shining down on her. Adam was still holding her hand, and even as she was being lifted onto the delivery table she continued to cling to him. She noticed the Entonox beside her which would give her some pain relief. She motioned towards it.

Adam handed her the mask and as Patricia inhaled the nitrous oxide and oxygen into her lungs the analgesia began to take effect. She felt totally light-headed as people moved around her. A midwife was examining her birth canal, assuring her that she'd nearly reached dilatation.

'Won't be long now before you can start pushing your baby out,' Adam said as he wiped a damp cloth across her forehead.

He was sitting beside her, his face close to hers. She gave him a weak smile as she tried to remember how long she'd known him. She motioned again for the inhalation mask as a strong contraction claimed her.

It was like being in a confusing dream. Where had Adam come from? He'd just materialised out of nowhere and could easily vanish again. She opened her eyes. He was still there. What would she do without him?

And now they were telling her to push. Patricia squeezed Adam's hand. His other arm was around her shoulders and she leaned against him, taking comfort from his strong body. He was like a rock that wouldn't break. She might break but Adam wouldn't. He was always going to be with her, wasn't he? He would never, ever abandon her. She felt so woozy, it was difficult to know what was going on…

'You've got a beautiful baby girl!'

The midwife was holding a white bundle in her arms, handing it to her. Patricia gazed in wonder at the little miracle. Her baby…this was her baby! She felt desperately tired but she'd never known such happiness as she felt at that moment.

She looked at Adam. He was standing up now and she had difficulty focussing through the bright lights. There was a crown of light around his head, making him look like one of those magnificent gods she'd read about in school who sometimes came down from Mount Olympus to live among the mere mortals like herself.

He leaned down towards her and smiled. 'Congratulations, Patricia! You were great!'

And then he kissed her on the cheek. His kiss, as light as a butterfly's wing, excited her. Her mind became clearer. She remembered she'd only known this man since this afternoon. What time was it now? Was it still today? It didn't matter. She felt as if she'd known him all her life.

The midwife, who was reaching forward to take away the baby for her routine tests, turned to look at Adam.

'And you were a great father,' she told him. 'So calm and helpful with—'

'I'm not the father,' Adam said quickly.

'Oh, I see.' The midwife looked embarrassed. 'Well, do you want to hold the baby for a few moments or shall I just get on with the tests?'

'I'd love to hold her, if that's OK with Mum,' Adam said, smiling as he opened his arms.

Looking up at Adam and her new daughter, Patricia felt a lump in her throat. It was such a beautiful sight!

'She's wonderful!' Adam said. 'Have you got a name for her?'

Patricia nodded. 'Emma, after my mother.'

'Your mother will be so happy.'

'She died when I was small,' Patricia said quietly.

'I'm sorry. But now you've got another Emma.'

His voice was, oh, so comforting she wanted to cry. The midwife was taking her baby from him now.

He leaned forward. 'Jane and Richard have just arrived and they're waiting for you in the postnatal section of Nightingale Ward. I've got to go, I'm afraid. Plane to catch back to the States.'

She reached out and grabbed his hand. 'Do you have to go?'

'I'm afraid so,' he said quietly. 'Jane and Richard will take care of you.'

He leaned forward and kissed her once more on the cheek before walking briskly away.

CHAPTER TWO

PATRICIA was enjoying the warmer weather after the relentlessly cold, stormy days of a typical Yorkshire winter. It was one of those spring mornings that made you feel good to be alive. As she unbuckled Emma from her car seat, she distinctly heard her first cuckoo of the year. That was always something that had excited her as a child when her father had taken her walking into the woods down there beside the river.

She kept her head bent to avoid bumping it on the low roof of her newly acquired but ancient Ford Fiesta as she extricated herself and Emma from the car. Holding her daughter against her, she pointed down the hillside.

'Look, Emma, that's where I used to play when I was a little girl. You're only six months old, but in a little while I'll take you into the woods and you can run about, watch the rabbits and make daisy chains, just like I used to do. If you listen carefully, you'll be able to hear the cuckoo.'

Emma smiled, revealing two perfectly formed, pure white milk teeth at the top and two at the bottom as she began chattering in her own distinctive baby babble.

'Shush for a moment, Emma. Can you hear it…?'

Emma had put her little head on one side as if to show her mummy that she understood. Her smile broadened before she continued in her baby-speak. Patricia pressed her face against her daughter's soft, blonde, sweetly smelling, newly washed hair.

'You heard it, didn't you? Let's make a wish, shall we? When you hear the first cuckoo in spring, your wish will come true.'

She remembered so well being excited when her father had told her that. So she would continue to impart the ancient myths to her daughter when she was old enough to understand, even though she herself didn't believe wishes came true any more. What would she wish for now if she still believed in fairies and Father Christmas? She smiled as she remembered her teenage wish had always been for a handsome man to share the romance of a lifetime with. He would have whisked her off her feet, totally captivated her and they would have married and had lots of babies...

Ben had been nothing like that, but at least she'd now got her wonderful baby. And she had her all-absorbing career which was something she knew she couldn't live without. Medicine and Emma were her whole life now. She'd given up on romance, if indeed it existed outside romantic novels, which she seriously doubted.

She'd tried so hard to convince herself that she was self-sufficient that she didn't want to admit there was anything more she needed. More time to herself, more money perhaps? Yes, it would be great to be able to buy her own place, instead of renting. The little terrace house Patricia was renting in the main street of Highdale would be a good start if she could find enough for a deposit and convince her bank manager that she would be able to keep up the mortgage payments. And some carefully chosen furniture would improve the place.

But in terms of emotional happiness she was completely fulfilled, wasn't she?

Patricia took a deep breath as she glanced around the garden she was standing in, taking in the long, sweeping drive she'd just driven up, the well-tended lawn interspersed with beds of spring flowers surrounding Fellside, the magnificent stone house that belonged to Jane and Richard. She could have been forgiven for feeling a pang of envy, but it wasn't the material trappings that economic stability brought so much as the safety of being in a permanent relationship where there were two parents to share the load of child-rearing and provide emotional security in the family.

She brushed aside the thought even as it sneaked into her consciousness. It was so much better for Emma that she should have one entirely devoted parent than two parents who were together simply for her sake. That's how it would have been if she'd gone ahead and married Ben.

'Hi, Patricia!' Jane had come out through the large oak door and was standing on the top step, a welcoming smile on her face. 'Hasn't Emma grown? Come on inside. Edward's dying to meet her. I thought this would be a chance to chat about sharing the workload at the practice before you actually start tomorrow.'

Jane's ten-month-old baby, Edward, looked up from the sitting-room floor where he was chewing the edge of the Chinese carpet and chortled happily.

'Ba-ba-ba-ba…'

'Yes, a little friend for you to play with,' Patricia said, putting Emma down on the carpet.

Mrs Bairstow, Jane's housekeeper, who had been carefully watching over Edward, frowned. 'I should be a bit careful, Dr Patricia. Don't take your eyes off Edward, will you? He can crawl now, you know, and if he decides to grab hold of little Emma's hair…'

'It's OK, Mrs Bairstow,' Jane said soothingly. 'We'll

watch both of them like hawks. You don't need to worry.'

Mrs Bairstow started to walk away. 'Well, I'll go and get the tea, then.'

As the door closed, Jane smiled across at Patricia. 'Mrs Bairstow doesn't approve of the way I put Edward on the floor. She came to look after us when I was twelve, soon after my mother died, and she still thinks I'm a novice where children are concerned.'

Patricia settled herself against the cushions of the squashy sofa. 'I remember meeting her that time I came out for a weekend when we were students and you lived up at Highdale House. She was definitely in charge of the place and I was a bit scared of her, to be honest. She ticked me off for not changing out of my wet jeans when we'd been over the fields one dewy morning. I must have been about twenty, but I remember feeling about six years old as I got up from the breakfast table and went upstairs to change.'

Jane laughed. 'Heart of gold she has, really,' she said. 'But she's convinced she knows best about everything so I try not to annoy her too much. When we started on the extensions to the surgery at Highdale Practice we had to incorporate the living quarters of Highdale House so Dad came to live with us here at Fellside. And where Dad goes, Mrs Bairstow follows. We did suggest she might like to retire and put her feet up, but she firmly squashed that idea. We're all very fond of her. She's part of the family—No, Edward, don't chew Emma's socks!'

She reached forward and, picking up her son, removed him to the far end of the room where there was a huge pile of toys. Picking up one of the bricks, she began building a tower. After three bricks had gone up, Edward smashed them down and laughed happily.

Patricia scooped up Emma who had started to cry. 'It's OK, Emma. Edward was only being friendly.' She looked across at Jane who was still squatting on the carpet, building another tower. 'So, doesn't anyone live up at the practice any more?'

'Maria, one of our community nurses, lives with her husband in the flat above the old stables and they keep an eye on the place at night. And our three-legged cat, Miriam, refuses to move house. We've tried bringing her down here but she simply goes back again, so Maria feeds her when we're not there.'

Jane stood up and went to the window. 'Oh, good! Adam's here!'

Patricia felt a moment of sheer panic, tinged with an indefinable sense of excitement. 'You mean…Adam Young?'

Jane turned back from the window. 'Well, don't look so surprised! He starts work tomorrow as well. I thought it would be good for all of us to get together and sort out how we're going to share the work. Didn't I tell you he was coming?'

Patricia shook her head. 'No, you didn't. I…er, I haven't seen him since the day Emma was born.'

'But you knew he was coming to work with us, didn't you?'

'Oh, yes. I remember being so thrilled when you and Richard told me the good news that both Adam and I had got the jobs we wanted. It was soon after I'd been settled into the postnatal section of Nightingale Ward, wasn't it?'

'We waited until we thought you were capable of dealing with it. But I wasn't sure how much you were taking in. And we've both been so busy during the last six months, we haven't had time for a chat. I knew you had enough to do, moving over to Highdale from Leeds, without me bothering you about work. How's everything down at your new home?'

Patricia gave Jane a wry smile. 'It's been a week since we moved in and I've still got unpacked boxes everywhere. Not enough shelves for my books, too much unwanted furniture from the people I'm renting it from…but I'm getting there!'

She paused. 'I was pleased you chose Adam over the other candidate. He was so…friendly and helpful to me when I was in labour.'

'So I heard. Jennifer Baxter, the midwife, told me she thought he was your husband— Adam! Lovely to see you again. Come and sit down. You remember Patricia?'

Emma had started to wail because she was confined in Patricia's arms. Patricia stood up as she tried to placate her daughter and found herself looking up into those brown eyes which had constantly flashed unbidden and unwanted across her inner consciousness since the fateful day she'd met him. Adam Young was even more handsome than she remembered!

Oh, heavens, she felt so embarrassed as he looked down at her!

He was smiling in such an enigmatic way that it made her wonder what was going on inside his head. Was he remembering how she'd clung to him, how she'd made a perfect fool of herself?

'How could I ever forget?' he said, in that cool, calm, velvety voice which had kept her going through the final pangs of her delivery. 'Although I'm not sure I would have recognised you in the street. I suspected you were tiny, but—'

'My grandmother used to tell me that diamonds came in little packages,' Patricia said quickly, her automatic response to remarks about her size. 'And I don't mind being tiny again, having experienced what it was like to weigh a ton.'

He put out his hand and touched the side of the arm that was curved around the wailing Emma. 'I think it suits you. So, this is the little madam who was causing all the fuss at Moortown General. What a beautiful little girl! May I hold her?'

'Please, do!' Patricia thankfully handed over her noisy, wriggling daughter.

Her legs were beginning to feel wobbly and she sat down quickly. Adam took the chair next to her and made clicking noises with his tongue as he held the crying baby on his knee. After a few moments Emma stopped wailing and stared at him, her blue eyes solemn as she seemed to be weighing up whether she liked this new person or not. Adam continued the clicking noises. She smiled and, laughing gleefully, reached forward with her plump, dimpled hand and grabbed the lock of dark brown hair that had fallen over his forehead.

'Ow!' Adam said, in a playful voice.

Emma giggled happily but let go of Adam's hair so that she could stroke the fine texture of his jacket. Edward crawled across and hauled himself up on Adam's trouser leg, trying to get in on the fun.

'I'm not surprised the midwife thought you were the father,' Jane said. 'You're a natural with babies.'

'It was such a quick delivery that there wasn't time to explain who anybody was until after Emma arrived,' Patricia said quickly.

'Were you there when your own daughter was born, Adam?' Jane asked.

Patricia felt a pang of a strange emotion she couldn't define as she listened, intrigued, for his answer.

Adam nodded. 'Yes, but it was a much lengthier labour.'

Patricia noticed that his voice was devoid of emotion and that he didn't appear to want to elaborate. She couldn't understand why the thought of him having a wife and child wasn't how she'd imagined him. Why had she hoped he would be single? Her fantasising about him during her labour had been brought on by the gas and air she'd been inhaling, but there was no excuse for her to continue living in cloud-cuckoo-land.

She'd already decided that she wasn't going to embark on a new relationship for years and years, if at all, so his marital status should be of no interest to her whatsoever. Adam had been someone to lean on when she'd felt weak, that was all.

So why did she keep on thinking she was attracted to him in a big way?

'How old is your daughter?' she asked politely.

He smiled and his voice took on a warm element of paternal pride. 'Rebecca is five. She lives with my ex-wife and her second husband near Moortown. That was one of the reasons I wanted to come back to this part of the world. With my hospital commitments in the States, I couldn't get over here to see Rebecca as often as I wanted.'

He broke off and lowered his voice. 'I think Emma is going to sleep.'

Patricia looked at her daughter's drooping eyelids. 'She woke up very early this morning so she's due for a nap. I'll go and get the car seat so that it will be easier to transfer her when I go home,' she said as she went out through the door.

She was glad to be alone for a few moments as she went down the stone steps and crossed the gravel drive. Adam's car—parked next to hers, she noticed—was a larger model than the small sporty affair in which she'd curled up on her way to hospital. As befitted a family man, no doubt. The thought that he wasn't single had depressed her, but her spirits had lifted when she'd heard his wife was an ex and had another husband.

As she unlatched the car seat she told herself she must stop the romantic nonsense before it got out of hand. She was on the rebound from Ben at the moment and not in a fit state to meet up with an attractive, personable, helpful man.

Back in the sitting room again, Patricia took Emma carefully from Adam's arms. She could smell the aroma of that same heady masculine soap she'd noticed on his hands when she'd held them against her face during her labour. Remembering her immodest behaviour that day, she could feel herself going red with embarrassment. Quickly she turned and strapped the sleeping Emma into the car seat.

What must he have thought of her? From what she could remember, she'd flung herself at him and demanded all his attention. She'd even asked him not to go and catch his plane! As soon as the opportunity arose she would apologise, explain that it had been the analgesia and her hormones playing her up.

Mrs Bairstow had arrived with the tea-trolley and Jane started to pour the tea.

'I'm going to take this little chap out of harm's way,' the housekeeper said, bending down to pick up Edward. 'Hot, scalding tea and babies don't mix. I'll take him into the kitchen and put him in the play-pen.'

'Here's Richard arriving,' Jane said, looking out

through the window. 'And Dad's with him. Richard and I take him out on our rounds sometimes. Dad likes to call in and chat to his old patients. Since he retired they're always asking about him so it's a two-way form of therapy whenever he goes to see them.'

'Doesn't he interfere with your methods of treating the patients?' Adam asked.

Jane laughed. 'You bet! But we usually manage to agree in the end. Dad has known some of the older patients for years and that counts for a lot when you're treating them. I'm often glad to take his advice. Modern technology is all very well, but we can learn a lot simply by listening to our patients.'

'I've found that giving them time to get things off their chests is always a good idea,' Patricia said.

'Exactly!' Adam said. 'That's one of the things I missed when I moved from general practice to work in hospital. There was never enough time to get to know the patients before they went away and you started all over again with someone else.'

'It looks as if we all agree on the main idea of the Highdale practice,' Jane said, as she handed Patricia a cup of tea. 'Give the patients all the time you can afford. If you've got a patient with a deep-seated problem, be it psychological or physical, you've to spend time finding out what's wrong. Never mind if the waiting room is full. That's why I'm so happy we've now got more staff.'

'Hear! Hear!' Richard said, as he came through the door.

'They've even had to bring me out of retirement,' Dr Crowther senior said as he slowly crossed the room to sit in his favourite chair by the fireplace. 'Hello again,

Patricia. Good to have you on board. You too, Dr Young.'

'The name's Adam, sir. And I'm very pleased to join the practice.'

Dr Crowther took a sip from the tea Jane had just given him. 'You didn't train at Moortown General like these other three, did you, Adam?'

'No. I trained in London, at St Celine's Hospital, went into general practice in Devon and then worked in America.'

Dr Crowther smiled. 'And at last you've had the sense to come and work here. You'll never want to leave Yorkshire, you know.'

'From what I've seen so far of the county, I think you're probably right,' Adam said politely.

He turned to look at Patricia and she felt the colour heighten in her cheeks.

'We've just been to see Alan and Diane Greenwood and their new baby,' Richard said. 'They're looking forward to meeting our two new doctors so I said one of you would go out for their next home visit.'

'Alan has multiple sclerosis,' Jane explained. 'So you can imagine how thrilled they were when Diane produced a lovely, healthy little boy last month.'

She turned to look at her husband enquiringly. 'Diane is coping OK, is she? It's a lot of work, having to look after Alan *and* the new baby.'

Richard's expression was thoughtful. 'She seemed tired. She was worried that she hadn't been able to get to the chemist for Alan's prescription of beta interferon. It's a couple of days overdue. I told her one of us would nip back this evening with some.'

'Yes, you do that, because Alan definitely needs it,' Dr Crowther said. 'He wasn't walking as well as the last time I saw him. That new drug is an absolute wonder. I was a bit sceptical when it was first tested but now I'm utterly convinced.'

Adam stood up, placing his cup carefully on a side table. 'Tell you what, why don't Patricia and I go out there now and deliver the beta interferon? That will kill two birds with one stone. Alan will get his medication and meet the new doctors at the same time.'

'That sounds like a good idea to me,' Jane said. 'Don't worry about Emma, Patricia. She'll be OK if she wakes up, with three doctors to look after her.'

There wasn't time for Patricia to feel apprehensive about the idea of being alone with Adam. She deliberately put herself into professional mode. This was simply a man she had to work with. She would have to get used to treating him like a normal human being instead of somebody she'd got an annoying crush on.

And the sooner she got rid of that romantic notion, the easier it would be to get on with her medical work to the best of her ability. Medicine was her life now— that and Emma. There was no place in her life for the emotional turmoil she was experiencing. It had to be totally eradicated and the sooner the better so she could get on with her own life!

As Adam drove his car along the winding country lanes, she glanced sideways at him, remembering with embarrassment how she'd snuggled against him across the gear shift of his small, rented car when she'd been in labour. His hard, muscular body had felt so comforting to her. She hadn't been able to get enough of him!

'I feel I owe you an apology for being so… er…forward the last time you drove me,' she said carefully. 'I felt so embarrassed afterwards when I thought how I'd behaved. You were so kind and patient with me. But you must have thought—'

'Think nothing of it.' He smiled. 'I was only doing what any medical colleague would have done. And you were in labour so you weren't expected to behave as you would normally.'

Patricia sank back into the passenger seat, wondering why that answer didn't satisfy her. He'd only been doing what any medical colleague would have done, had he? Deep down, had she hoped he would say that in spite of the fact that she'd been looking like a beached whale and behaving as if she'd been out of her mind, he'd been deeply attracted to her?

And where would they have gone from there, in the unlikely event that he'd come up with such an inexplicable answer? She gave herself a mental ticking-off. Really, her ability to fantasise hadn't changed since she was a child! Here was a gorgeous hunk of a man, obviously not short of money by the look of this new car, with his child being safely cared for by his ex-wife, whereas she was permanently up to her eyes in nappies and baby responsibilities.

He would turn every uncommitted female head for miles around so she'd better stop dreaming! What could he possibly see in her?

'It looks like we're nearly there, from the brief description Richard gave us,' Adam said, as he slowed down the car. 'This could be the little road we have to take. What do you think, Patricia?'

'It's got to be this one. Richard said it was simply a glorified farm track.'

Adam turned into the muddy little road and proceeded with caution over the potholes. 'You can tell they've had a rough winter up here among the fells. We'll both have to get used to that in a few months' time.'

'I don't mind the winter in the Dales,' Patricia said. 'When I was a child, I used to love coming home after a day in the cold and sitting by the fire, toasting crumpets on a long brass toasting fork, listening to the wind howling down the valley outside—' She broke off, realising she was talking to him as if she'd known him for years. It was exactly how she'd felt when he'd been taking care of her in hospital—a nice, warm, comfortable feeling that she wanted to build on.

'I know I'm going to love it up here,' he said quietly, as he pulled the car to a halt in front of a long, low building. 'I was born in the Essex countryside and I've always preferred to live in the country. My years in America were simply…' He paused, as if searching for the right words. 'Simply a necessary break from my life in England. It's great to be back.'

She turned to look at him and their eyes met. 'It's all about roots, isn't it? The little things you remember from childhood, the memories that you never forget and you want to pass on to your children.'

His eyes were quizzical. 'Children? So you and your partner…?'

'I was speaking in the abstract,' she said quickly. 'Yes, one day in the far distant future I'd like to have a brother or sister for Emma, but not for a long time.'

'So you and your, er, partner…?'

'I haven't got a partner. Emma's father and I split up months ago.'

She was watching his reaction but he was giving nothing away as his eyes held hers.

'I guessed that was the case but I didn't like to ask too many questions when you were in labour.' He put his hand over hers. 'You were very brave to go through your pregnancy on your own.'

She swallowed hard. The touch of his fingers was unnerving her and removing all her resolutions to stay detached from him. 'Not really. Lots of women do it. And as I saw it there was no alternative.'

Patricia stopped speaking as she saw the door of the house opening. 'We'd better go in.'

Alan Greenwood was leaning on a stick as he waited for them by the open kitchen door. A tall man in his late thirties, he had a pleasant, smiling face, but the effort of coping with his multiple sclerosis had taken a toll on his once muscular body.

Adam smiled and held out his hand. 'I'm Dr Adam Young and this is Dr Patricia Drayton. We've brought your medication.'

Their patient's careworn face brightened. 'That's very kind of you. Come in and meet my wife.'

Alan turned and walked carefully through into a cosy but chaotic living room. Damp baby washing was hanging from an airer fixed to the ceiling and piles of dry, washed clothes lay heaped on every chair and surface.

A tall, thin woman about the same age as her husband looked up from breastfeeding her baby and gave them a wry smile.

'Excuse the mess. I can't seem to get anything sorted since Matthew arrived. Chuck some of those things off a couple of chairs and sit down. It's good to see people from the outside world. I'm Diane, by the way. Would you like a cup of tea? Matthew's nearly finished his feed and—'

'No, thanks,' Patricia said quickly. 'We just popped in to say hello and deliver the medication.'

As she'd been speaking she'd been assessing the situation. It was obvious that this new mum, marooned up here with an invalid husband, was having a difficult time. She watched as Diane took the baby from her breast and put him over her shoulder. She looked worn out but was struggling valiantly to appear as if she was still in control.

'Come on, Matthew, give me a nice loud burp and then I can put you down and get on with some of this ironing.'

'Endless, isn't it?' Patricia said gently. 'When you've got a baby the work never stops piling up. I've got a six-month-old baby myself and I never feel as if I've finished.'

Diane's tired face creased into a smile. 'Really? But yet you're managing to work as well, while I can't even get myself down to the shops. You know, before Alan and I got married I went travelling round the world by myself for a couple of years.' She gave a nostalgic sigh. 'Looking at me now, I bet you wouldn't believe that, would you?'

'Oh, but I would,' Patricia said firmly. 'I can tell you're a strong character. It takes guts to live up here amongst the fells and look after your husband and baby.' She paused. 'Is there anyone who helps you, I mean family and so on?'

Diane shook her head. 'Mum's too old to come trekking up here and I'm an only child. Besides, I can manage.'

'But if somebody gave you a couple of hours to yourself, that would be nice, wouldn't it? I can arrange for a home help, perhaps twice a week. She could help with the housework and you could go down to the shops by yourself—'.

'Now, that would be a good idea!' Diane said evenly.

She lowered her voice, glancing over towards her husband. Seeing that he was deep in conversation with Dr Young, she opened up.

'Sometimes I feel so trapped, Doctor. I love Alan and baby Matthew but…I was never any good at keeping house and…' Her voice trailed away as the threat of tears became obvious.

Patricia stood up and, gently removing the baby from Diane's shoulder, she placed her over her own. The baby gave an obliging burp.

Diane rubbed her hand over her eyes. 'There's a good boy! Wouldn't do it for your mum, would you?' She turned watery eyes towards Patricia. 'Thanks, Doctor. A home help would be great!'

'Don't worry, Diane. I'll get that fixed this week if I can.' She picked up a packet of disposable nappies. 'Matthew feels a bit damp. I'll change him and then we can put him down for a nap.'

'I'm going to fix a home help for Diane,' Patricia told Adam as they drove off down the rutted track a little later. 'She's reached breaking point and as she's not only caring for her baby but also for a husband with an incurable disease, I think I can persuade the social services that she's a deserving case.'

'Absolutely!' Adam turned out into the main road and increased his speed. 'I could see you were getting Diane's confidence as the two of you whispered together.'

'How did Alan seem when you talked to him?'

'He seems to be coping extremely well. He obviously adores his wife and child, but he's completely dependent on Diane. You were quite right to insist she gets some help.'

'Exactly!' She looked across at him questioningly as he slowed the car and pulled onto the grass verge.

He switched off the engine. 'I'm glad we've got a chance to talk by ourselves. There was something I wanted to say to you before we start working together.'

Patricia watched, mesmerised, her heart beginning to beat rapidly as he leaned across towards her.

'I knew, as soon as I saw the way you were watching me earlier this afternoon with that strange look on your face, that you were worried about the day that Emma was born…the way you behaved as if you'd known me a long time. And then when you broached the subject as we were coming up here…'

'It's OK, Adam, you've explained that you were only doing what any other colleague would have done. I've put it out of my mind and—'

'But have you really?'

He reached across and took both of her hands in his. 'You're still embarrassed, aren't you? You acted out of character and you can't forgive yourself.'

She was excited by the touch of his fingers. 'Yes, I was embarrassed when I thought back over what had happened,' she said slowly. 'But not any more. Now that I know how you feel about me.'

'Feel about you?' His eyes were tantalisingly close to hers and she could see nothing but tenderness in them. 'I don't think I know, myself, how I feel about you, because I've only just met the real you today. But I have to say I like what I see.'

Adam leaned closer and brought his lips down upon hers. She savoured the moment before he drew away, looking down at her to gauge her reaction.

He gave her a rakish grin. 'That wasn't what I intended when I stopped the car. I simply wanted to clear the air so we could work together without any unresolved problems from our first meeting hanging over us.'

She looked up at him, trying to disguise the fact that she'd been totally enthralled by his kiss. Her lips were still parted, more in hope than in anticipation, but he recognised her silent invitation.

His second kiss deepened as he folded her into his arms. A sensual electric current was running down her spine, stirring up the dormant passions deep inside her which she'd forgotten for so long. Oh, how she missed the closeness of a virile body pressed passionately against hers, but warning bells were ringing in her brain. This wasn't part of her plan, to become embroiled with another man before she was barely over her last disastrous liaison.

Patricia stirred in his arms, trying to gain some control over her treacherous body. Adam must have recognised her dampening signals because he moved back against his seat.

He pushed the wayward strands of dark hair back from his forehead. 'I'm not usually so over-friendly when I meet a new colleague, but…'

His sensual lips curved slowly into one of his heart-rending smiles. She felt quite weak as she realised she was still reeling from the sensations he'd stirred up inside her. This had to be pure lust she was feeling, didn't it? This longing to escape into that dream world where she could entwine herself in Adam's arms and lose herself in the passions that would envelop them both.

Patricia swallowed hard, knowing she'd got to get a grip on her emotions. 'I think we should be going back. I've got to reclaim my daughter and Jane will be wanting to start explaining our work at the practice.'

He switched on the engine just as a farm vehicle trun-

dled into sight over the hill. It was inevitable that they
had to wait until it passed them and then follow slowly
behind it down the hill.

'Jane will be wondering what's happened to us,'
Patricia said, staring through the windscreen at the wisps
of straw that were now floating down from the back of
the truck onto the bonnet of Adam's car.

'She won't realise we had to stop and have a high-
powered conference on our future working practices,' he
said in a whimsical voice.

Patricia laughed. 'We had to clear up the embarrassment factor.'

'Would you say we were about quits now?'

'Something like that.'

'So it's not going to be a problem?'

She shook her head. 'Absolutely not.'

Patricia shifted in her seat as she put herself back into
professional mode so that she would be able to face Jane
and Richard and make a serious contribution to their
discussions about the medical work of the practice.
There would be no problem about working with Adam.
The problem would be all those times when they weren't
working! If they were alone together with no restrictions
on their time, how would she react if he kissed her
again?

Would she be able to resist the temptation of going
along with her treacherous body rather than listening to
her head?

In front of them, the farm vehicle turned into a field.
She breathed a sigh of relief as Adam put his foot down
harder on the accelerator. The high stone walls of
Fellside came into view.

Neither of them spoke until they were walking together up the wide stone steps at the front of the house.

He put a hand lightly on the back of her jacket in the small of her back.

'Are you OK?'

She paused for a moment to look up into those expressive eyes. Had he any idea how hard she was finding it to bring her emotions under control?

She smiled. 'I'm fine.'

Jane was opening the door. Patricia hurried ahead.

CHAPTER THREE

IT WAS going to be OK. She'd worked a whole week with Adam and hadn't let her carefully planned public face slip in any way. She'd been totally professional— in fact, positively cool towards him on occasions.

Patricia banished the intrusive thoughts from her mind as she brought up the medical notes of her next patient on the computer screen. There had been a two-minute gap between patients, which was unusual. Lucy, the receptionist, had said this was her last patient of the morning. She read through the notes and checked the accompanying X-rays whilst deciding on a course of treatment for her elusive patient.

Maybe Mrs Catherine Sutton had got tired of waiting and gone home. It had been known since the influx of new patients. This was one of the problems they were going to have to consider now that the practice was expanding. Jane had said that her old patients had disliked the appointments system when they'd tried to introduce it a few years ago, but it was beginning to look as if it was time for a change.

A new kind of patient, drawn from the housing estate or the holiday village, now attended the practice. Attuned to the efficient ways of urban medical practices, like the one where she'd worked in Leeds, they didn't want to sit around gossiping with old friends, content to see one of the doctors whenever they were free.

Lucy poked her head round the door. 'Sorry for the

delay, Patricia. Mrs Sutton's in the loo. She shouldn't be long. Would you like another coffee while you wait?'

Patricia smiled. 'No, thanks, Lucy. I'll soon be having my lunch with Emma.'

She sank back against the chair as the door closed. Lucy had been so helpful during her first week. Although she was probably only about ten years older than Patricia, she'd mothered her along through all the small problems that always arose when you didn't know the layout of a practice. Lucy had told her she was a trained nurse who preferred to work part time so that it fitted in with her family life, two children at school and a hard-working husband to look after.

In fact, everyone she'd come in contact with had been most helpful. Adam had seemed to get the hang of the place on the first morning. He was out on his rounds now, no doubt charming the entire female population. She'd noticed the admiring expressions on the faces of his female patients as they looked up at him—not that she'd been watching with any special interest, of course!

She glanced out of the window at the beautiful garden that surrounded the practice and blended so well with the hills beyond. She could see the road that led up from the valley. Recognising the familiar black car that was just about to turn into the surgery car park, she had to work hard to quell the leap of excitement she was experiencing in the pit of her stomach.

This was what happened when you spent every evening washing baby clothes, ironing or cleaning the house. She ought to get out more! Perhaps this weekend she could strap Emma in that new contraption shaped like a glorified military backpack and head for the hills.

A flustered, middle-aged lady burst into the room.

'Sorry to keep you, Dr Drayton. I got caught short. I've been waiting such a long time and—'

Patricia smiled at the newly arrived patient. 'No problem, Mrs Sutton. I'm sorry you had to wait so long. Do sit down. How's the wrist? Would you like to move your fingers for me?'

The patient's notes had told Patricia that Catherine Sutton had slipped and fallen on the wet floor of the bathroom in her home on the new housing estate. She'd fractured her right scaphoid, one of the small bones involved in the articulation of the wrist.

'Your fingers are a good colour, Mrs Sutton, and there's no swelling,' Patricia said, as she examined the part of the hand that protruded from the plaster. 'This happened a week ago, didn't it?'

'Yes, it was really silly of me. I was simply reaching for a towel when I slipped. I put my hand out to save myself and that was it.'

'According to your notes, you've had a few breaks over the years, haven't you?'

Catherine Sutton gave a wry smile. 'Well, I'm fifty-five and you can't expect to sail through life without a few knocks, can you?'

Patricia smiled back reassuringly. 'That's a good, positive attitude.' She paused. 'Now, I've been studying your X-rays and I think we're going to have to do something about your bone density. In other words, your bones are a little bit fragile and break more easily than they should. I'm going to make an appointment for you to see a rheumatologist at Moortown General.'

Mrs Sutton frowned. 'A rheumatologist? I haven't got rheumatism, have I?'

'No, you haven't,' Patricia said gently. 'From studying your X-rays, I think you may have a condition called osteoporosis, which fortunately is quite treatable. Doctors and scientists have been studying it for some time now and are coming up with some excellent remedies. I'd like you to see a consultant. He'll probably give you a bone scan which—'

'How will he do that, Doctor?'

'It's very easy. You simply sit in a chair while a radiographer examines your heel with a special machine. It only takes a few minutes.'

Mrs Sutton shifted on her chair, looking puzzled. 'But why the heel?'

'Because that's a dense, bony area and will give an accurate idea of what's going on in the rest of your bone structure. I'll make an appointment with the hospital and they'll let you know when it is, Mrs Sutton.'

Her patient was smiling as she stood up. 'Thank you, Doctor. Can I come in and chat to you about it when I've been to the hospital? I get all flustered when I'm having a hospital appointment and I can't seem to take it in as well as when I'm here with someone who'll answer all my questions.'

Patricia smiled. 'Of course you can. Take care of yourself and don't worry.'

Someone tapped on the door. Probably Lucy. She called out, 'Come in.'

'Oh, sorry. I didn't know you had a patient with you.'

Adam was standing in the doorway and she felt an annoying pink flush spreading over her cheeks.

'That's OK. We've just finished.' She turned back to Mrs Sutton, who said her goodbyes and bustled towards the door.

'I was hoping to find Jane,' Adam said, as soon as they were alone. 'I can never remember which one of you is in here on which mornings.'

Well, it was good that he thought of her and Jane in the same way!

'It should be Jane this morning but baby Edward had a bit of a temperature so she phoned and asked if we could swap mornings. If it's something infectious she doesn't want Ann, her part-time mother's help, to come in, pick it up and take it home to her own children. Anything I can help you with?'

'Not really. I'll get in touch with Jane at Fellside. She knows the case I'm dealing with and I thought we could have discussed it now.

Patricia gave a wry smile. 'Instead of which there was only the novice here.' She stood up. 'Look, I've got to dash. I need to pick up Emma from my sister's. She's going shopping this afternoon so I mustn't be late.'

He put out a hand to detain her as she hurried to the door. 'I'm glad I saw you because I was going to have to give you a ring.'

'What about?'

He grinned. 'Don't sound so fierce.'

She smiled, her hand on the doorknob. 'Sorry. But I really do have to go.'

She knew she had to escape as quickly as possible because, just by being in the same room as Adam, she could feel herself thawing out and forgetting all her good resolutions to the contrary!

'You may think this is a bit of a cheek, but I wondered if you'd help me out this weekend.'

Her heart did a somersault but she kept a straight face. 'In what way?'

'Well…' He paused and looked at her with the most captivating smile. 'If you really don't fancy it you will say, won't you? You mustn't feel you're obliged to do it.'

'I would never do that,' she said evenly. 'Believe me, I never do anything I don't want to.'

But she knew that whatever this mystery assignment was she would probably love to do it if it involved being with Adam!

'Good! The fact is, Lauren, my ex-wife, wants to go away for the weekend and she's asked me to have Rebecca. I'm absolutely delighted, of course, but it's ages since we spent so much time together and I don't want her to get bored. So I thought if you could bring Emma round on Saturday afternoon and stay for early supper, that would brighten up the weekend for her. Rebecca loves babies, apparently.'

Patricia grinned. 'So Emma and I are to be the Saturday entertainment, the cabaret, so to speak, are we?'

'You'll have to tell me your fee, of course,' he said solemnly.

'Double on Saturdays, but special reduction if you feed us. I'll have to check my daughter's diary, of course, but if she's free then we'll be happy to come along.' She could hardly disguise just how happy she was not to be contemplating the entire weekend alone with Emma, the ironing board and the washing machine.

'I'll phone you later with directions.'

So this was the so-called cottage Adam had spoken about! Some cottage! Four, five bedrooms at least! Patricia brought the car to a halt and turned off the engine. Looking up at the dormer windows of the upper storey, birds' nests visible under the overhanging eaves, she thought it was the most dreamy place she'd seen outside one of those glossy magazines about living a well-heeled lifestyle in the country. It had everything.

Early flowering roses rambled round the entrance to the porch, ivy tangled on the ancient stone façade.

She tried to contain her amazement as she saw Adam coming out onto the porch at the top of the stone steps at the front of the house.

'How on earth did you find this place?' she called, as she hauled Emma out from her car seat. 'It's absolutely idyllic.'

He smiled as he came towards her, his feet crunching on the gravel. 'It's adorable, isn't it? I saw it in a magazine when I was still working in the States and I knew I just had to have it for Rebecca and me.'

He turned to introduce the little girl who was hiding shyly behind his back, her small fingers gripping the sides of Adam's jeans.

'Rebecca, this is the little baby I told you about. Say hello to Emma.'

Slowly, Rebecca came out from behind her father's back and looked up at Patricia who was holding Emma.

'Perhaps if I could hold Emma?' Adam said, holding out his hands towards Patricia.

Emma fixed him with one of her serious expressions as he held her. Gently bending his knees, he brought her down to the eye level of the little five-year-old.

Rebecca's face creased into a smile. 'Ah! Isn't she small, Daddy?'

'You were as small as that once, Rebecca.'

'Was I? Did you have to carry me all the time?'

'Until you could walk. This is Emma's mummy, Patricia.'

'Hello, Mummy Patricia,' Rebecca said solemnly. 'Can Emma walk?'

'Not yet. But if we put her down on the floor she'll try to crawl. Shall I show you?'

'Ooh, yes!'

Carefully, Patricia put out her hand and was thrilled that the little girl took hold of it as they went into the house, Adam following behind with Emma.

The house seemed to wrap round them in a warm welcome.

'You've really made this place seem like a home already,' Patricia said, looking around the cosy sitting room at the front of the house. 'How long have you been in here?'

'I moved in three weeks ago, but it was already furnished, which suited me fine as I hadn't any furniture of my own. The previous owners have moved to a small retirement apartment in Florida so most of the items here were too big. You can tell it's been a real family home so I didn't have to work too hard to make it habitable.'

'Habitable! It looks like you've been here for years.' She paused. 'You seem to belong here.'

He gave her a long, slow smile. 'I feel as if I belong here. For the first time in my life I've put down roots...I think. Of course, I haven't got everything I need but— Yes, in a moment, Rebecca, I'll put the baby down. Let me find a suitable space... Here will be nice and safe, away from the door.'

Gently Adam lowered Emma down to the carpet, laying her on her back. She gurgled up at him and grabbed his finger.

'What a charmer you are! May I have my finger back? Thank you. I want to make Mummy a cup of tea. Rebecca, take good care of Emma, won't you?'

'Of course I will. Come on, Emma, show me how you can crawl.'

Emma obliged by rolling onto her tummy and doing the squirming movements with her arms and legs that looked more as if she were swimming and didn't actually propel her across the floor.

Rebecca lay down on her tummy and copied Emma's movements. 'Look, Emma. If you just pull yourself along like this...'

Patricia smiled happily as she watched Rebecca playing big sister to Emma. Her spirits were lifting as she waited for Adam to return from the kitchen. She glanced around the comfortable sitting room. Squashy cretonne-covered sofas and chairs nestled among lovingly polished side tables. One wall was entirely devoted to bookshelves, another taken up by a large bay window, its casements open to give a better view of the garden and allow the heady perfume of the roses to pervade the room.

Was this what family life was like on Saturday afternoons when there was a mummy, a daddy and two small children? If it was as idyllic as this she wouldn't mind trying it! But not with her baby's father, not with Ben.

'I've got shortbread biscuits for the girls,' Adam said, carrying a large teatray into the room and placing it on a round, antique table in the bay window. He looked at Patricia. 'Emma can chew on a biscuit, can't she?'

Patricia smiled. 'Try stopping her!'

They walked down to look at the stream at the bottom of the garden when they'd finished their tea. The sun was beginning to drop down in the sky towards the hills across the valley. Patricia stopped suddenly.

'Can you hear the cuckoo?'

Adam smiled. 'I heard a cuckoo this morning when we were having breakfast and— Yes, listen, Rebecca, remember I told you to make a magic wish when you heard the cuckoo this morning?'

The little girl nodded solemnly and closed her eyes.

'Oh, you can only have a wish when you hear the cuckoo for the first time,' Adam said.

Patricia looked across at him enquiringly. 'Maybe two if you're a five-year-old,' she said in a wheedling tone.

He laughed. 'OK, but make this one a good one, Rebecca.'

The little girl had a serious, almost adult expression as she opened her eyes again. 'I wished I could come and live here with you, Daddy.'

The silence that followed was utterly poignant. Patricia glanced at Adam and saw that he was temporarily lost for words.

'I think Mummy wants you to live with her and Tony for most of the time,' he said carefully.

Rebecca pulled a face. 'I don't like Tony. He's horrid! He shouts at me all the time.' She gave a big sniff. 'He doesn't shout at Rowan and Theo.'

Adam reached down and picked up his small daughter, cradling her in his arms. 'That's because the twins are only two, sweetheart. You're a big girl now and—'

'But you don't shout at me.'

Patricia could see that this awful exchange was becoming unbearable for Adam. She could imagine how he was feeling, knowing that his daughter wasn't happy in her home life.

'Will you show me where you saw the tadpoles you were telling me about, Rebecca?' she asked. 'Emma would like to see them, wouldn't you, darling?'

The temporary distraction helped to ease the tension. They searched the rocky pool at the edge of the stream where the tadpoles had been when Adam had first moved in. There was no sign of them but a couple of small frogs put in a surprise appearance, which meant that

Patricia could explain the fascinating story of how tadpoles turned into frogs.

The subject of Rebecca's home life was happily forgotten and the talk at the supper table in the kitchen was mostly about frogs. Adam had found a high chair for Emma which had been left by the previous owners and Rebecca wriggled happily on top of two cushions placed on a kitchen chair.

Patricia spooned puréed carrot and cereal into her daughter while Adam served up scrambled eggs for his daughter. Reaching across for a cloth to mop up some spilled apple juice, Patricia's eyes locked with Adam's. In spite of the chaos around them, she felt a sudden inward peace as his charismatic gaze held hers.

Just for this moment she felt they were like a real family, and the electric current of emotion running between herself and Adam was so tangible it almost took her breath away. She found herself wishing, completely irrationally, that this state of affairs between them could last longer than a few hours.

As if her own thoughts had transmitted themselves to Adam, she heard him speaking in a husky voice.

'We're not going to get a very peaceful supper, you and I, if we sit down now at this sticky table and try to eat what's left of the scrambled eggs,' he said, his eyes still locked with hers as if totally sensitive to her reaction. 'If you like, I could cook us some supper when the girls are asleep.'

She felt a tremor of emotion sweeping over her at the thought of an intimate supper just for the two of them. It would give her a chance to get to know this fascinating man without being interrupted by their medical work or their demanding children. And did she really want to uproot herself from the warmth of this family situation to return to her little house and spend the evening catching up on her domestic chores?

'I'd like that,' she said quietly.

She was aware that Rebecca had paused in her non-stop chatter and was listening in to the adult conversation.

'Emma can go to sleep in that cot I found when I was upstairs, playing in one of the bedrooms,' the little girl said excitedly. 'Can I help you to put her in it, Patricia? And then I can sing ''Baa, Baa, Black Sheep'' to help her go to sleep. Do you know that song? Shall I sing it? ''Baa, Baa, Black Sheep, have you any wool…'''

Patricia smiled as she listened to the pure, sweet, lilting, young voice. 'That was lovely, Rebecca,' she said as Rebecca stopped singing and leaned forward, almost toppling off her chair as she waited for Patricia's verdict. 'Of course you can put Emma in the cot. Would you like that, Emma?'

Emma gave a wide grin and reached out to grab the hand that Rebecca was holding out towards her.

'I think you've made the right decision,' Adam said quietly. He reached inside the freezer. 'Chicken casserole OK?'

She nodded. 'I can see you're a great cook.'

He gave her a wry grin. 'With a little help from the local supermarket.'

She noticed he was studying the instructions on the packet as he moved over to the oven. His brow was furrowed in concentration as if he were about to perform an important surgical operation. The tip of his tongue was clamped firmly between his teeth in the attitude she'd seen him adopt as he studied a patient's notes on the computer.

She felt a surge of affection rising up inside her and

at the same time a moment of sheer panic. What was she doing, allowing herself to mellow towards a man she hardly knew? But it was difficult to ignore the warm glow of desire she felt whenever she was with him.

'That should do it,' he said, slamming the oven door. 'Come on, Rebecca, it's time for your bath.'

His daughter slid off the cushions, laughing as she landed on her bottom on the floor. 'Emma needs a bath as well.'

Adam looked across at Patricia. 'Do you want Emma to have a bath?'

Patricia smiled as she stood up and began to unstrap Emma from the high chair. 'I think it would be a good idea if I splashed away some of the stickiness before she sleeps.'

Rebecca was jumping up and down with excitement. 'Can I help bath Emma? Tony doesn't let me into the bathroom when the twins are having their bath. He says I'll get in the way.'

'Of course you can help me,' Patricia said, taking hold of the small hand that was held up trustingly towards her. 'Now, you'll have to show me the way upstairs, Rebecca.'

'Here, let me carry Emma,' Adam said, taking the baby from her usual place on Patricia's hip. 'We'll need to put sheets on that cot. There's masses of linen in the airing cupboard, left behind by the previous owners. I haven't got around to sorting it yet, but I presume that as they had a cot there'll be some small sheets.'

Bathtime was a riot of laughter, wriggling and splashing. Patricia held on firmly to a giggling Emma as Rebecca soaped her skin. At one point, as Patricia wiped her own face with the back of her hand, she found bubbles from the baby foam sticking to her chin.

Adam laughed and reached forward to wipe the foam away. It was another tender moment when their eyes met. The touch of his sensitive fingers on her skin unnerved her. She could feel herself melting with a deep longing and realised that she could barely wait to be alone with him. The thought of the evening stretching ahead was as tantalising as it was fraught with danger— the danger of losing her head and going against all the promises she'd made to herself.

But the feelings of warmth towards Adam flooded through her.

There were more giggles when Patricia dressed Emma in one of Rebecca's clean nightdresses, which enveloped her completely. It was a pink and white flowered cotton garment with ruched sleeves and lace around the bottom that trailed like a train beneath her feet.

'Ah! Emma looks like a beautiful fairy,' Rebecca said, the affection and warmth she felt towards the baby palpably obvious. 'Can we put her in the cot now, Patricia?'

Adam reached forward and held his hands out towards Emma. 'I'll hold Emma while you put the sheets on her cot, Patricia. You probably understand these things better than I do.'

Patricia was aware that he was watching her as she searched through the shelves of the huge airing cupboard.

'You've got enough sheets to start a hotel,' she quipped as she pulled out a couple of small ones.

Turning round, she smiled up into Adam's eyes and the melting feeling intensified. She began to wonder if her fingers would allow her to put the sheets on the cot if Adam were to stand and watch her in her present emotionally unsettled mood. The effect of those dark, deeply sensitive eyes had a profound effect on her and she could feel her legs beginning to turn to jelly.

She noticed that Emma's eyes were beginning to close as her little daughter snuggled against Adam's chest. Emma and Rebecca would soon be asleep and then she and Adam had the whole evening ahead of them.

'There's a single bed in the room with the cot,' Adam said quietly. 'You'd be much more comfortable staying the night there than having to uproot Emma after supper. What do you think? You'd be most welcome to stay, Patricia, and I wouldn't have to worry about you driving around these narrow country lanes in the dark. It's entirely up to you.'

His dark eyes were totally enigmatic. The ball was in her court. She told herself that it was merely the friendly, courteous gesture of a good host, but her emotions were dictating otherwise. Would it be possible to sleep across the landing from this desirable man who was putting her emotions in turmoil?

Her sensible self told her that it would be perfectly possible if she kept her emotions in check. All she had to do was pretend she didn't fancy him rotten, and behave like a good house guest, retiring early to the bed next to her baby daughter before she got carried away by being alone with him.

She was glad that Rebecca had already left the bathroom and was already rehearsing 'Baa, Baa, Black Sheep' as she waited at the cotside for Emma. If she'd heard what her father was now suggesting, the cute little minx would have already begun persuading her to stay.

'I'm not sure if Rebecca's cradle song will put Emma to sleep or make her want to get up and dance,' Patricia said, playing for time as she tried to decide whether she should take up Adam's kind offer of hospitality, know-ing how she felt about him.

Adam laughed, breaking some of the tension between them. 'Come on, let's go and see.'

Patricia hesitated. 'It's kind of you to offer me a bed,' she heard herself saying. 'It would make sense to settle down for the evening and not have to go out again.'

Adam nodded his approval. 'Good. It's the end of a long, busy week and you need to relax.'

As she followed him through into the bedroom, where Rebecca was singing all the nursery rhymes she'd ever learned, she told herself that Adam was right. This was just what she needed. A relaxing Saturday evening with a good friend.

The thought that sprang into Patricia's mind as she went down into the kitchen after the girls had finally fallen asleep was that she and Adam were alone at last. She watched as he lit the candles in the silver candelabra he'd brought in from the dining room.

'I thought we should make an occasion of it,' he said easily. 'This is the first supper party I've given since moving in here.'

He turned round and took a bottle of champagne from the fridge. Peeling off the foil, he eased out the cork. She took the glass he was holding out towards her.

'Happy house-warming!' Patricia said, as they clinked glasses. Then she noticed the mess on the table.

'Let me sort this out,' she said, putting down her glass and moving the remains of the children's clutter over to the sink. 'Where do you keep your cutlery?'

'In the drawer by the sink, but pick up your drink and come and sit down first. We need to relax and turn into real people again after all that mummy-and-daddy work.'

As she moved over towards the old open fireplace where a couple of easy chairs stood on either side, Patricia realised she'd enjoyed playing mummy to Adam's daddy. It had been great fun. But this was simply make-believe. Real parents weren't like this, doting on their children and then hurrying away downstairs to drink champagne.

Or were they? She took a sip of her champagne as she looked across the fireplace at Adam.

'This is a good way to spend a Saturday evening,' she said shyly.

His gaze held hers. 'There's something about Saturdays that makes you feel you should do something special, so I'm glad you're here with me to make it a special occasion.'

'Well, I've had to cancel a number of engagements,' Patricia joked, 'but it was worth it in the end.'

Adam smiled, and she could feel her heart melting towards him. She couldn't remember when she'd felt so emotionally moved by anyone.

The inner voice inside the sensible part of her brain was telling her to take it steady, but she deliberately overruled the idea. This was one Saturday evening when she planned to enjoy herself and take full advantage of being with the man who was beginning to mean so much to her. It couldn't do any harm as long as she reverted to her sensible self later…could it?

'I missed cosy evenings like this when I was over in America,' Adam said, picking up the champagne bottle and moving across to top up her glass.

His hand touched hers as Patricia held out her glass and she had to suppress a shiver of emotion that would have made her fingers tremble.

He turned away. 'The bright lights of the city are all

very well in small doses but you can't beat a quiet evening in with an interesting friend.'

'Your divorce must have been something of a wrench,' she said carefully, when he was safely back over the other side of the fireplace and her pulse was calming down again. She hesitated before asking the question uppermost in her mind. 'You don't have to tell me, but I wanted to ask why you and your wife split up.'

She watched anxiously as Adam frowned. 'If you don't want to talk about it...' she said as the silence lengthened.

'I'd like to tell you. I would probably find it therapeutic to discuss it with someone as...er...as sympathetic as you. I just don't know where to begin.'

'How about the beginning?' she said gently.

His eyes held a haunted expression as he turned them upon her.

'At the beginning Lauren and I were very much in love—well, I thought we were, but maybe she was fooling me even then. After Rebecca was born, I thought we had everything. I'd finished my GP training and was enjoying my work at a practice in Exeter. Lauren had gone back to work at the firm of accountants she'd been with before Rebecca was born. One of us used to take Rebecca to the local nursery every day. And then...'

He seemed to be grappling with an unpleasant memory.

'And then the dream vanished,' he said quietly. 'Everything we'd built up since I met Lauren when I first moved to the Exeter practice from my London hospital...everything collapsed. It was one of my partners at the practice who took me out for a drink and said he thought he felt it his duty to tell me something I should know.'

She swallowed hard as she waited for the inevitable unpleasant story to unfold.

'I remember being in this noisy pub and then, little by little, as Harry began to tell me, this incredible story...which I refused to believe at first...the crowded room seemed to go silent. There was still the same noise, I believe, but my ears could only home in on what he was telling me. At one point I felt I couldn't take any more. I asked him not to tell me any more—that it was all a lie—but he continued anyway...'

He put both hands to his face as he remained silent for a few seconds. Patricia found she was holding her breath as she waited.

'Harry told me he'd known Lauren since they were at school together in Exeter. She'd always been a flirt and enjoyed having lots of boyfriends. He himself had taken her to bed a few times in their teens and he knew of other friends who'd enjoyed her favours, to put it in an old-fashioned way. Nobody who really knew her ever thought she'd settle down with one man and get married. She worked as hard as she played and she'd become a successful accountant. Apparently, when I moved down from London and started going out with her, everyone assumed it would be just another of her temporary affairs.'

Adam clenched his fists and his expression changed from misery to anger. 'If only I'd known half of what Harry told me that night I wouldn't have gone ahead and asked her to marry me...or would I?'

He looked across the fireplace towards Patricia, his eyes moist with emotion. 'I thought she was the most beautiful, talented woman in the world so I probably wouldn't have listened to him if he'd tried to put me off before we married. It's quite true that love is blind,' he finished off in a hoarse voice.

'So was Harry telling you that…?'

'Apparently, she was having a full-blown affair with a man called Tony Crawford. You may have heard of him. He's a big name in the building trade. You've probably seen his adverts selling executive properties and retirement homes. A self-made man—he started off as a bricky—he likes to flash his money around and enjoy a luxurious lifestyle. Harry said it definitely wasn't a meeting of minds, but he'd certainly captivated Lauren during the last few months. He expected it would fizzle out but he thought I ought to know the facts.'

'What did you do?'

'I went home and asked Lauren if it was true. At first she denied it and then she started laughing and telling me it didn't mean anything. She admitted she didn't think she could play the part of faithful wife any more. She liked her freedom to roam. I told her she could have as much freedom as she liked now because I wanted a divorce. I insisted we would share custody of Rebecca, who was two at the time. She agreed. I moved out and made plans to leave the town where so many people had known more about Lauren than I had.'

'So you escaped as far as you could by going over to the States.'

He nodded. 'I applied for a surgical post in New York and hard work helped me to forget. But the image of my little daughter was always with me and I used to be sad when I had to leave her after a brief spell in England. Lauren and Tony moved up to Yorkshire when Tony expanded his building interests to this area. He was responsible for building the new housing estate and the holiday village.'

'He must be quite wealthy by now.'

Adam gave her a wry grin. 'Probably worth more than a country GP. He's had an enormous house built on the hillside overlooking Moortown and Lauren's enjoying a much easier life than she had with me.'

'Yes, but is she happy?'

He shrugged. 'What's happiness?'

Patricia smiled. 'That's a deep question. I used to think I was happy when I was engaged to Ben but now…'

'Does Ben come to see Emma?'

She hesitated. 'He came once, when she was a few weeks old, but…but he hasn't been since.'

Patricia found herself remembering the whole unpleasant incident but she didn't want to talk about it and spoil the rapport that had built up between them.

'One day I'll tell you about it, but not now,' she said. 'It certainly seems as if we're both in the same boat. Ben cheated on me and that was before we were even married.'

She broke off, sniffing the air as the distinct smell of overcooked food began to pervade the kitchen.

'I think your casserole is about to leap out of the oven,' she said, jumping to her feet, glad of an excuse to forget about the past and enjoy the wonderful present.

Adam laughed as he sprinted across to the oven and flung open the door. 'Done to a turn! Or rather a turn and a half. Does madam like her casserole well browned on the top?'

Patricia smiled as she handed him the oven gloves hanging from a hook beside the cooker. 'Looks perfect to me.'

The broccoli was also overcooked but it didn't seem to matter as they leaned across the table towards each other, exchanging snippets of conversation, talking about the books they enjoyed reading, the music they liked best and theatre outings they'd made before they'd got embroiled in child-rearing.

She was thinking happily about how much they had in common as she pushed her plate to one side and leaned back in her chair, watching him across the table.

He passed her a basket of fruit. 'Dessert?'

Patricia took an apple and bit into it, finding that her eyes were still riveted on this fascinating man. She wanted this evening to go on for ever. She'd had two glasses of champagne and realised that she was mellower than usual, but she was still in command of all her senses. Still able to know what she was doing.

When Adam leaned across the table and took hold of her hands she grasped his with equal firmness.

'Let's take our coffee into the sitting room,' he said quietly.

She nodded. 'What about the washing-up?' She gestured to the debris.

He smiled. 'Leave it. Let's not spoil a good evening.'

Patricia leaned back against the cushions of the sitting-room sofa a few minutes later, feeling a delicious sense of unreality sweeping over her. As Adam handed her a small, delicately proportioned cup of coffee she smiled up at him.

Their hands touched again and she knew she was lost. Yes, it had been a brilliant idea to stay the night. It would be even more wonderful to spend the night with Adam. She watched him as he stood with his back towards her, selecting the soothing, romantic music that was soon enveloping them.

'Rachmaninov?' she asked.

He nodded. 'His second piano concerto.'

'I love it.'

'So do I,' he said, his voice husky with emotion.

He put his cup down on the side table and leaned towards her. She found herself compelled to join him in the middle of the sofa. It was as if the whole evening had been leading up to this moment when they could finally be together.

Patricia turned her face up towards his, willing him to kiss her. And when his lips came down on hers she was unable to stifle the blissful sigh that escaped her. She turned to look up at him. The tenderness in his eyes was, oh, so tantalising. She found herself mesmerised, drawn to reach up to him as if by some magnetic force. He took hold of her hands and gently pulled her to her feet.

Slowly, Adam gathered her into his arms. His eyes were questioning as he brought his lips down against hers as if trying to sense her reaction. She could feel delicious sensations in the depths of her body.

He held her tightly against him as his kiss deepened. She parted her lips and a strong frisson of arousal ran through her as she felt the sensual touch of his tongue. All her resolutions were slipping, slipping away as she felt his hands caressing her.

It had been so long since she'd submitted to a man's caresses. Should she force herself to put an end to this wonderful feeling of closeness or should she abandon all her sensible ideas and...?

As his caressing hands touched her breasts Patricia gave up all thoughts of the consequences. She wanted to stay in Adam's arms until she'd satisfied this longing in the only way possible. She could feel his hard manhood pressed against her body and her longing for fulfilment increased.

'Yes, Adam,' she found herself whispering.

As he scooped her up into his arms and carried her out of the kitchen and up the stairs she nestled her head against his shoulder. The door to the master bedroom was wide open. She'd glimpsed it earlier when she'd put Rebecca and Emma to bed in their rooms across the corridor, and she'd marvelled at the sumptuous furnishings, the rich, brocade, floor-length curtains, the deep soft pile of the carpet and the enormous four-poster bed…

But now her mind barely registered her surroundings as Adam laid her gently on the bed. He pulled her into his arms and Patricia gave herself up to the rising tide of pleasure that was sweeping her along…

Patricia slowly opened her eyes and looked up from the pillow. Adam was propped up on his elbow, looking down at her, and he gave her a gentle smile. 'I didn't plan this.'

She stretched out her arms and pulled him closer. 'I didn't offer any resistance, did I? It wasn't what either of us planned but…'

She stopped. Don't get in too deep. You've gone too far already but, oh, it was worth it.

'But what?' he said, his voice husky with emotion.

'But I enjoyed being with you even if I'd told myself I wasn't going to get involved with anyone so soon after my disastrous affair with Ben.'

He leaned back against his pillow. 'Believe me, I understand exactly what you're going through. After Lauren cheated on me it was a long time before I could even look at another woman.'

'I invested so much emotional energy on Ben before he threw it all back in my face,' she said quietly. 'I doubt I would ever dare to make that amount of commitment again for fear that…'

Her voice trailed away as the tears threatened to spill from her eyes. She swallowed hard, but he had taken her in his arms again and she revelled in his caresses with renewed desire. This time when he entered her she was totally relaxed, knowing of the heavenly sensations ahead that would drive her wild with longing before she reached the final ecstatic climax…

Patricia tiptoed out of Adam's bedroom, giving a final look back at the sleeping figure. He looked so handsome, so desirable, his naked body draped across the rumpled sheets of the four-poster. She crossed the corridor and went into the smaller room where Emma was peacefully sleeping. She'd stopped the late night feed a couple of weeks ago and was relieved to find that Emma always slept all night. But she often wakened early in the morning.

That would be a good time to make her escape. She'd said her goodbyes to Rebecca when she'd put her to bed, and the little girl hadn't expected her to stay the night. She would leave a note for Adam explaining that it was better if she went home before Rebecca started asking questions. That way she wouldn't become too involved, would she?

As Patricia climbed between the cool sheets of the single bed she knew she wasn't fooling anybody, least of all herself. She was already too involved, already hopelessly entangled with this man.

She thought about their love-making… Yes, that was what it had felt like—making love. It hadn't been just a physical act to satisfy her sensual desires. She had given herself totally and Adam's responses had been more than she could ever have dreamed about.

So now what was she going to do about it? How was she going to come back to earth and live in the real world where men could shatter your dreams and leave you in the depths of unhappiness?

CHAPTER FOUR

As SHE drove along the narrow lanes above Highdale, Patricia had time to think about the events of last Saturday. Since that wonderful evening, only a few days ago, when she and Adam had made love, she'd tried so hard to resume a professional working relationship with him.

She could excuse herself for breaking her resolutions on that one occasion but she knew that if she allowed it to happen again it would be even harder to resume a normal relationship between them. Adam, too, had seemed at pains to behave in an ultra professional way. But every now and then she caught him looking at her with a strange, enigmatic expression.

Was he regretting the fact that they'd behaved like ardent, passionate lovers? Was he afraid that she would have misinterpreted his tender murmurs of endearment to signify that they should become more involved?

With a determined effort she put the thoughts from her mind. The patients had to come first and she had to give them her full concentration. She turned off the main road and followed the track down to a farmhouse. The kitchen door was wide open. As she stepped out of the car she could feel the warm rays of sunshine on her face. She'd even dared to come out without a jacket, and the cool cotton skirt and blouse felt liberating after the restricting layers of the winter and early spring.

Yes, summer was almost upon them. When she'd dropped off Emma at Helen's that morning, her sister had said she was going to do some gardening and the children would be able to help. That meant that Emma would now be sitting in her pushchair, watching her cousins help their mother. Even though Helen was a brilliant mother, Patricia doubted whether much work would be achieved with the help of four-year-old Gemma and two-year-old Tom! But she was glad that Emma was going to be enjoying the fresh air. She must try to take her out again this afternoon, but she would take the pushchair and stick to the good, easy paths because that baby carrier she'd bought weighed her down too much.

A couple of bossy ducks waddled up from the muddy duckpond and crossed the farmyard in front of her, cackling loudly at a group of hens who scattered, clucking indignantly at being ousted from their own territory.

A plump, fiftyish woman appeared in the doorway, her arms across her ample, flower patterned, apron-covered bosom.

'Thank you for coming, Doctor. My boy's not well this morning.'

As Patricia went across the farmyard she could see the lines of worry etched on Mrs Watson's face. Her only son, Craig, was twenty-seven now but she still called him her boy. It had been an awful shock to her when his kidney disease had been diagnosed last year. From being a sporty, athletic young man, full of life, he'd been reduced to a semi-invalid, forced to spend every night hooked up to his dialysis apparatus.

'He's been sick and he's got those tummy cramps like he had before Dr Montgomery sent him to hospital last month,' Mrs Watson said wearily.

Patricia put a comforting hand on the worried mother's shoulder. 'I'll go and have a look at him.'

'He's in his bedroom, Dr Drayton. Said he couldn't

face getting up this morning. I'll get on with my work while you're in there because he says he doesn't like me fussing around.'

Craig was lying very still, breathing heavily. Patricia went over to the bed and took hold of his hand. Tired eyes looked up at her warily.

'I've been really careful about sterilising all the equipment every morning, Doctor,' he said in a weak, despondent voice. 'Last month when I had to go into hospital, Mr Smythe, my consultant, tore me off a strip for not doing the sterilisation properly. He said that was why I'd got that awful peritonitis. Please, don't tell me it's come back again, after everything I've done.'

'Let me have a look at your stomach, Craig,' Patricia said gently.

She put her hands over her patient's abdomen, palpating carefully around the area where the tube had been inserted. There was a definite irregularity there. She straightened up and looked down at Craig. He was an intelligent young man. She could give him the facts.

'I think your tube may have moved into an awkward position inside you, so the dialysis isn't as effective as it should be. There may even be a blockage, but don't worry—we can put it right,' she said.

Craig pulled a wry face. 'That would account for the fact that the alarm on this wretched machine kept going off every few minutes in the night. Honest, I didn't get a wink of sleep. God, I hate it—all this wretched paraphenalia and…!'

His voice trailed away, the threat of tears not far behind, as he gestured with his hands towards all the apparatus that cluttered up his small bedroom. The football cups and flags adorning his walls served only as a poignant reminder of his former life.

'I don't feel like a man any more,' he said, almost under his breath, and this time he couldn't hold back the flow of tears that spilled down his cheeks. 'What girl would ever want to take on a freak with a tube stuck out of his stomach?'

'Craig,' Patricia said gently, as she took hold of both his hands. 'You're still—'

'I'm sorry, Doctor.' He was swallowing hard as he tried to regain his composure. 'I haven't broken down before. Mustn't get sorry for myself. But sometimes everything—'

'You've been a brilliant patient, Craig. This is another temporary setback. I'm afraid it's going to mean another visit to the hospital but, hopefully, you should only be in for a couple of days while they check on your tube. I'll get the ambulance to take you in this morning.'

'OK,' he said in a resigned tone. 'When do you think they'll be able to get me a kidney transplant?'

'Craig, I wish I knew,' Patricia said carefully. 'It's impossible to predict when you'll be lucky. In the UK, the average waiting period is more than a year, I'm afraid. You've been on the waiting list about thirteen months now, haven't you? So we'll just have to hope that—'

'How do they decide who gets the kidneys from this waiting list, Doctor?'

'Well, it's not so much a waiting list as a pool. When the kidneys come in, a group of four or five people who may fit the kidney type are called to the transplant hospital—in your case, Moortown General. They take into account how long each patient has been waiting and then the most suitable person is selected. Someone with a rare blood type such as AB-negative might be the only per son of his type waiting for a kidney, but he may have to wait a long time for that type to come. You're not in a rare blood group so there's a good chance that you'll get your transplant within the next few months, but I can't promise anything.'

'I hope so! Aagh!'

Patricia leaned forward. 'Another cramp?' she asked in a sympathetic voice. 'I'll phone the hospital.'

'How was Craig Watson?' Adam asked her, as he came out of his consulting room.

'I've had to have him admitted to Moortown again,' Patricia said, putting down her medical bag on one of the chairs in the empty waiting room. 'I think the dialysis tube has shifted internally and there may be a blockage.'

Adam frowned. 'I wish we could get that transplant.'

'It can't come soon enough. He's getting very fed up. Did you have a busy morning?'

He nodded. 'The last patient has just gone. Richard and I never stopped. It's a good thing we've reinstated the appointments system, otherwise the patients would have been queuing outside in the road. There were several people from the holiday village with gastric problems. I hope there's nothing wrong with the water supply. Richard's gone down there to have a look.'

He folded his arms and leaned against the side of the doorpost. 'I'm really looking forward to my half-day off.'

'I'm sure you are,' she said lightly, reaching down to pick up her bag as she made for her own consulting room. She would check to see if there were any messages for her before she went off to pick up Emma.

'Patricia, I was wondering…'

She turned to look at Adam. A smile was hovering on his lips.

'It's such a beautiful day, I thought I might go for a walk by the river. Would you like to come with me?'

Her heart was pounding. 'What about Emma?'

He raised one eyebrow in surprise. 'Well, obviously, Emma would have to come with us. You said you had one of those rucksack-type baby-carriers.'

She smiled. 'I've only used it once. It's terribly heavy, and when you add Emma's considerable weight I feel as if I'm on a military manoeuvre. I've only used it once and I was exhausted after about a mile.'

'That's because the manufacturers don't make them for petite girls like you. Don't worry. I'll put it on my back and carry Emma—that's if you'd like to come…'

She hesitated. Here in the surgery, there had been a certain tension between them since their idyllic night together. So maybe a friendly walk together would put their relationship back on a purely platonic footing. Which would be beneficial for both of them, wouldn't it? Beneficial from a work point of view, anyway!

'Yes, I'd enjoy a walk by the river,' she said lightly. 'It's a lovely day out there.'

'It would be a shame to waste it,' Adam said, in the same conversational tone. 'The sooner we get out there the better. How about I pick you up in about an hour with a picnic lunch?'

This time she didn't hesitate. The thought of a picnic beside the river with Adam was much more enticing than a lonely meal at the kitchen table.

'Sounds great!'

*   *   *

Emma was propped up in a padded high chair at the end of Helen's kitchen table, her face smeared in chocolate pudding, when Patricia arrived.

Her sister reached for a cloth to wipe Emma's face. 'They were all three hungry, so I fed them early. Emma won't need any more lunch.' She lifted her niece from the chair. 'So you can put your feet up this afternoon— or were you planning to go out?'

Patricia put Emma on her hip. 'I might go for a walk by the river. It's such a lovely day,' she said quickly.

'You're not going to try out that contraption again, are you? I thought you were going to try and sell it.'

'Well, actually, there's a big strong man who's offered to carry it for me,' she replied.

Helen gave her a knowing smile. 'Not that dishy doctor you work with, the one who helped you through your labour? What's his name…Dr Young, isn't it?'

'Yes, Adam Young. Anyway, don't start reading anything into this. It's simply that it's a nice day, we both happen to have the afternoon off and—'

'And you look like you can't wait to get out there with him. I promise I won't jump to conclusions but I'll expect you to keep giving me a progress report.'

Patricia shifted her daughter to the other hip as she made for the door. 'Helen, there isn't going to be any progress. I'm not risking getting into any more serious relationships. Remember, I told you after what Ben did to me that I—'

'I know what you told me then, but a girl can change her mind if she—'

'Not this girl!' Patricia said, as she went out to the car.

As she strapped Emma into her seat she knew that her protestations were as much to convince herself as her sister. Helen was right. A girl could change her mind, but not so soon after she'd been betrayed. It was much too soon to trust her own feelings while they were still reeling from her experience with Ben.

There had been barely time to put Emma into a clean outfit and pull on her own jeans and T-shirt before Patricia heard Adam's car arriving outside her house. She stuffed the last of the washing into the machine and pressed the 'on' switch before making her way to the door.

'Hi! Come in.' As she held open the front door then led the way through to the kitchen she couldn't help thinking how good Adam looked in casual clothes. She loved his open white polo shirt, revealing just enough manly chest to make her feel weak at the knees with memories of that wicked evening.

'We're ready.'

Adam's tall frame seemed to fill the tiny kitchen. It was the first time he'd been to her house and she was acutely aware of the contrast between his spacious home and her little shoebox.

'Mind your head on the low beam,' Patricia said. 'When I rented this place, the estate agent said it was a nice little starter home, very compact.' She gave a wry laugh. 'It's big enough for Emma and me, but whenever we have anyone else in the house it seems positively crowded.'

'I think it's very cosy. And it's got bags of atmosphere. How old is it?'

'The estate agent told me this row of terrace houses was built in the middle of the nineteenth century to house farm labourers. It's got very solid stone walls.'

'Certainly has.' Adam was tapping at the walls as he made his way to the back door that led from the kitchen into the pocket-handkerchief-sized garden.

'Nice south-facing garden.'

She laughed. 'You sound like the estate agent. At least I don't have to mow a lawn. This garden area was always used to grow potatoes and cabbages in the old days, I'm told, but the people who own it had those large flagstones put down to save labour. It may be functional but I think it looks rather stark and boring. I'll have to do something to brighten it up when I get the time.'

'You could put out some large terracotta pots with plants in to brighten it up,' he suggested.

'They're terribly expensive.'

'I've got a spare one in the conservatory that would start you off.' He stepped out into the warm sunlight. 'Yes, it would look good in this corner.'

'Oh, I couldn't possibly—'

'Please. The people I bought the house from left far more garden ornaments than I need. I'll get it round to you some time.'

'Well, thank you very much, then.' She picked Emma up from the rush matting under the kitchen table. 'Come on, darling. We're going for a walk.'

Patricia couldn't help laughing as she fixed the baby-carrier on Adam's back.

'It's not really your style,' she said, as she fastened the last buckle.

He gave her a mischievous grin. 'It's functional. We've come out for a country walk, not a fashion parade.'

They were standing in the riverside car park. An elderly couple walked past and smiled at Emma.

'What a lovely baby you've got,' the woman said to Adam. 'How old is she?'

'Seven months,' Patricia said quickly.

'Ah! You must be very proud of her.'

'Oh, I am,' Adam said, obviously enjoying himself.

He started walking towards the stile that led to the riverside footpath. Patricia followed, checking that Emma was comfortable on Adam's back. She was gurgling and crowing in her own distinctive baby language and seemed happy enough. Patricia hoisted one of the picnic bags over her arm. Adam was carrying the other one, which was filled with Emma's bits and pieces, slung over his shoulder above the straps of the baby carrier.

'I feel a bit like a packhorse,' he said with a wry grin. 'We'll settle down by the river and eat the food as soon as we can.'

'I know just the spot,' Patricia said. 'I used to picnic by the river when I was a child...there it is!'

It certainly was an idyllic spot. Set away from the main path, on the very edge of the river, it was shaded by low, trailing willow trees. The soft, dry, springy turf, warmed by the sun, was comfortable to sit on.

'Aren't the bluebells lovely?' she said, pointing to the blue carpet that surrounded them.

Adam was trying to spread a disposable paper tablecloth on the ground but Emma, lying on her stomach beside him, had other ideas. She gurgled with delight as she crunched the edges between her fingers until she managed to tear it.

Adam laughed. 'OK, you win, Emma. Who needs a tablecloth?'

He held out a packet of sandwiches towards Patricia. 'Ham and pickle.'

'Great! I'm starving!'

She leaned back against an oak tree as she watched Adam eating his sandwich and amusing her daughter by pretending to take away the paper tablecloth. Emma was laughing and grabbing hold of the paper every time

Adam pulled it away from her. The dappled sunlight that filtered through the trees was putting highlights into his dark hair. She tried to quell the warm rush of affection she felt towards him, but without success. How could she watch his tenderness towards her daughter without feeling moved?

There was no harm in that, was there? She looked out across the river, watching the diamonds of sunlight dancing on the ripples.

'I used to picnic here with my dad,' she said quietly, as the fond memories came rushing back. 'My mother died of leukaemia when I was seven, so Dad was left to look after Helen and me. Helen's five years older than me so she was more independent and used to want to play with her friends all the time. Dad and I used to go off on our own for long walks at weekends. I think it helped both of us to cope with Mum not being there.'

'Is your father still…?'

'No, he died when I was ten,' she said quickly.

His eyes registered deep sympathy. 'That must have been awful for you. So who looked after you then?'

'My grandma, my dad's mother. She always used to say she couldn't forgive her son for leaving us completely alone, but I understood why he…' She stopped, embarrassed, realising that she'd been rambling on as if Adam knew the whole awful story.

'I'm sorry. I don't usually like to talk about it but you're such a sympathetic listener. You see…' she took a deep breath '…my dad committed suicide.'

He reached forward and pulled her gently towards him. Emma, caught in the middle of them started protesting as she began to squirm her way onto Patricia's lap. For a few moments Adam's comforting arms surrounded both of them before he pulled away.

'I can't imagine how you coped with the terrible loss of your father, coming so soon after your mother's death.'

For a few moments she found she couldn't speak. She rocked Emma gently against her, comforted by the feel of that warm little person who was her own flesh and blood and also by the obviously sincere sympathy that Adam was showing towards her. Surely there wouldn't be any harm in telling him the true story.

She took a deep breath. 'I was the one who found him,' she said, quietly. 'I remember waking up early one summer morning and going down the passage to Dad's room. He didn't sleep much after Mum died and he was always awake. They had been very much in love and Dad never got over her death. If there was time we used to walk down to the river from that white house up there on the other side of the valley.' There was a lump in her throat as she pointed high above the river.

'That's where I was born and where I lived until I was ten and had to move in with Grandma in Moortown.'

'Tell me what happened that morning,' he said gently.

She took a deep breath to steady her voice which had become rather croaky. 'Dad wasn't in his room. I noticed his bed hadn't been slept in so I went downstairs, thinking he might have sat up all night. Sometimes he did that when he couldn't sleep for thinking about Mum.'

She paused and Adam waited, his dark, expressive eyes full of sympathy.

'He wasn't downstairs so I went outside and decided to see if he was in the garage, mending the car or something. I pulled open the doors and then...I could see him sitting in the car...just sitting. I thought he must have fallen asleep. I remember I couldn't breathe properly when I went in to see if he was all right. But he wasn't. I felt so scared when I saw him because—'

'Don't go on, Patricia,' Adam said softly. He reached forward and wiped her damp cheeks with a white linen handkerchief. She could smell some faint masculine scent as he brushed his hand across her face.

'I think it's helped to talk about it,' she said, as she recovered her composure. 'And, look, it's sent Emma off to sleep. I'll get her blanket out of the bag. She'll sleep more comfortably on that.'

'Here, let me do it.' Adam laid a hand on her arm. 'You need to relax and take it easy after remembering all that trauma.'

She watched fondly as he settled Emma under a tree next to them.

'It's a long time since I talked so much about the sadness in my early life,' she said, as Adam settled himself on the grass beside her. 'I managed to adapt to life without my parents, but it was never the same again. I think I had to grow up very quickly because my grandmother found it difficult to cope with losing her only son and then having to look after his daughters.'

'It must have taught you how to deal with unhappiness in later life,' he said. 'That was why you were strong enough to come through the break-up of your relationship with Emma's father so competently.'

Patricia turned to look at him. The tender expression on his face unnerved her. All this talk of her past sadness was softening her resolve to hold Adam at arm's length. There was nothing she wanted so much at this moment than to nestle against that strong chest and dissolve into tears.

She swallowed hard. 'I'm trying to cope with my split from Ben but sometimes, especially if Emma is being fractious or I'm overtired, I find it so hard. And then the only thing that helps me is to remember how deceitful Ben was and how breaking up with him was the only thing I could have done.'

'What did he actually do?'

She didn't want to talk about it. It would bring it all back. But then, seeing the sympathy in Adam's face, she felt compelled to share her awful secret.

'It was supposed to be a celebration,' she began, in almost a whisper, trying to be as dispassionate and objective as she could as the memories flooded back.

'A couple from the GP practice in Leeds where I worked had got engaged and had invited the staff and their partners to a party. Ben had promised to come up from London to accompany me. Two days before, he phoned to say he had to be on duty that evening.'

Adam shifted his position so that his arm was against her back, cushioning her from the hard bark of the tree. Patricia leaned back against his arm, enjoying the comfort of the closeness of his body and trying not to acknowledge the fact that it was more than just the comfort and sympathy that was appealing to her senses. Whatever it was, it was making the ordeal of telling her story much more bearable.

'I remember thinking that it was strange that Ben, being a consultant, couldn't have arranged cover for himself on the one night I needed him. Anyway, I was terribly busy and I didn't have time to brood about it.'

Unconsciously, she settled herself closer against Adam, drawing strength from his strong, muscular body.

'The day before the party, I did a pregnancy test. My period was a couple of weeks late and I'd been speculating about one particular occasion when I'd had a gastric upset which I thought might have affected the efficacy of the Pill.'

Patricia drew in her breath as she remembered how she'd gone into a state of shock as she'd read the result of the test.

'There was no doubt—I was pregnant. I had very mixed emotions, but one thing became clear. I had to discuss the situation with Ben, and not just over the phone. So I excused myself from the dinner and caught a train down to London.'

'So you didn't tell Ben you were coming?'

She shook her head. 'No, as I say, I was in absolute turmoil. I couldn't think straight and I didn't want to spring it on Ben over the phone. I thought he would be thrilled by my surprise visit but...' Patricia hesitated. Could she go on without dissolving into tears?

Adam's arm encircled her shoulders and he stroked the side of her bare arm in what was obviously meant to be a friendly, encouraging gesture. Momentarily, she forgot the anger she'd felt when she'd discovered what Ben had really been up to on that evening when he'd supposedly been on duty.

'I let myself into his flat with my key, planning to get some rest before he came home from the hospital. There was soft music coming from the bedroom. I thought he must have left the radio on. I went along the hall and opened the bedroom door. There was a heaving mound in the bed. I remember. I screamed with shock and horror, not wanting to believe my eyes.'

Adam pulled her closer against his side. Patricia revelled in the warm rush of security that enveloped her.

'It was almost ludicrous when Ben pulled himself away and turned to look at me,' she said quietly, anxious to finish her story so that she could enjoy the sensual warmth of Adam's comforting arms. 'I remember thinking he looked grotesque.'

'And the girl he was with?' Adam prompted.

'I didn't stay long enough to meet her. I simply walked out while Ben was searching for his dressing gown. I remember looking back and seeing him running down the steps into the street, begging me to come back. I found out afterwards from a mutual friend at the hospital that she wasn't the first girl to warm Ben's bed while I was away.'

'And what about the news you were going to tell Ben?'

'I decided that would have to wait until I'd reassessed the situation. When I'd calmed down I knew that I didn't want to have anything more to do with him. OK, he was the father of my unborn child. He had a right to know that but I would tell him in my own good time.'

'Which was?'

She smiled. 'I phoned him when I was about six months pregnant. First of all he wanted to know if I could prove it was his. That was the final straw. I told him that unfortunately it was but I had no desire to meet him again. If he wanted to see his baby he would have to do all the running about.'

'And did he want to see his baby?'

'During that first phone call he said he wasn't sure what he wanted to do. He said perhaps we ought to get married. I said that was out of the question. I would inform him when the baby was born and that was all.'

'So has he seen Emma?'

'Just once. He came up to Leeds for the day when she was a few weeks old. Emma was in a fractious mood. I was still breastfeeding her and I think she'd picked up on the fact that I was over anxious that day. Anyway, she threw up over his posh, consultant-style suit and he was furious. It was obviously one of his really expensive ones. He said he would stink the first-class carriage out all the way back to London.'

In spite of herself she found herself amused by the memory of Ben standing in the middle of her flat, holding out Emma towards her as if she were a piece of something he'd scraped off his shoe.

'I told him to call in at the nearest department store to buy a new outfit off the peg and he was horrified. We started having a row and Emma howled louder than ever, so I asked him to leave. That was the last I heard of him.'

'So he's not really the family type, is he?'

Patricia twisted in his arms so that she was facing him. 'I would say that was the understatement of the year.'

'I think you had a lucky escape.'

His warm breath on her face and the faint scent of his distinctive aftershave, coupled with the sympathetic expression in his eyes, were playing havoc with her resolutions. The comfort he'd given her as she'd been recounting her story had been an invaluable help.

How different this wonderful man was from Ben! Here was a real man, a real family man… She checked the thought as soon as it entered her head. She mustn't allow her tender feelings for him to affect her judgement where permanent relationships were concerned. For the last few days she'd been trying to re-establish the idea that they were just good friends, but being so close to him now brought back all the wonderful memories of their idyllic evening together. How could she forget all that and return to a platonic relationship?

Then, when Adam spoke next, it was almost as if he were reading her thoughts.

'Patricia, I've been wanting to tell you how much I enjoyed being with you last weekend,' he said, his voice husky with emotion. 'Working with you the last few days in the surgery, it's been so difficult to resume a normal working relationship and—' He broke off, looking down at her, his eyes pleading with her for some reaction to his dilemma. She felt relief flooding through her to know that he'd gone through the same emotions she had.

'It was exactly the same for me,' Patricia said. 'Every time we had to work together, with people around us, watching…it was so difficult that—'

'That's why I felt we had to get away together and clear the air. We had a fabulous evening last Saturday but…'

She felt a shiver of apprehension. 'But what…?'

'I couldn't help wondering during the last few days if you were regretting it.'

Patricia hesitated. 'How could I possibly regret such a wonderful experience?'

He breathed a sigh of relief. 'That's what I hoped you would say.'

'I still feel a bit battered and bruised after the way Ben treated me,' she began carefully, 'so I know I'm not ready for a serious relationship but—' She stopped, wondering how she could possibly explain how she felt about him.

Adam's eyes held real tenderness as he smiled down at her. 'I know what you're trying to say. Just because two people spend the night together it doesn't mean they're making a serious commitment to each other.'

She nodded. 'I think that's what I'm trying to say.'

'But it's perfectly possible to have a light-hearted romance with someone you're attracted to, isn't it?'

Patricia smiled up into those dark eyes and felt herself melting inwardly. Even as his warm lips claimed hers she was still trying to convince herself that this was a simple liaison that wasn't affecting her deeply. She could cope with the turmoil of emotions inside her, couldn't she? But not now. For the moment she was going to abandon her struggle and enjoy the sensations that were claiming her whole body.

As his strong hands caressed her arms, Patricia gave an involuntary sigh of pure desire. He held her against him as they lay down on the soft, mossy slope beneath the tree. The overhanging leaves gave them total seclusion from the rest of the world. All she could hear was the rushing of the river and the occasional call of a blackbird to his mate. If this wasn't heaven she didn't know what was.

She cuddled against him as his tantalising fingers caressed her breasts and she moaned as the depth of her desire threatened to overwhelm her. She was losing all control, longing for the ultimate state of sensual oblivion she'd achieved with him the first and last time they'd made love together. But her sensible self was trying to make itself heard above the crescendo of her passion. She couldn't go on like this, throwing caution to the winds and making it obvious that she adored him.

Apart from any other considerations, this wasn't the ideal setting for them to become wildly amorous. If someone strayed off the main path and witnessed the spectacle of the two doctors making love by the river in broad daylight...

Patricia pulled herself away, trying hard to get her breath back. Adam, too, was almost gasping for breath as they called a halt to their amorous encounter.

He gave her a rakish grin. 'You're thinking about the

headlines in the newspaper, aren't you? LOCAL DOC-
TORS CAUGHT IN COMPROMISING…'

'Don't!' She was running a hand through her rumpled
hair. 'Don't even think about it. What a scandal that
would be!'

He held out an arm so that she was simply leaning
against the tree with him in an upright position. As she
leaned against him, she was trying not to admit to herself
how much she loved him. Love! Was this really love
she was feeling? Reluctantly, she had to recognise that
an emotion that pulsated through her whole being like
this couldn't be anything else.

With a shock, Patricia realised she'd never felt like
this before. Never even in the first months of her affair
with Ben when he'd wined and dined her, showered her
with expensive presents and spoiled her to such a degree
that it had been impossible to separate gratitude from
genuine affection. She'd never before experienced this
heady rush of tenderness towards another man.

And she wanted it to continue for ever…which was
precisely the reason she should be trying to call a halt
now before it ran away with her, before Adam's feelings
for her began to wane and their relationship inevitably
broke up.

Patricia drew in her breath. Was it possible that something which was affecting her so profoundly could stay
as a light-hearted affair? If she was very careful, it might
be. She would take one day at a time and not look too
far ahead.

At the precise moment she was deciding that the only
thing she could do was not to make a decision but to
float along as lightly as she could, she became aware of
the shrilling of Adam's mobile.

He groaned as he pulled it from his pocket. She

watched him frowning as he took the call. Suddenly, as he listened he became animated. Now he was smiling.

'Lauren, you mustn't worry,' he was saying gently. 'I'll help you all I can… Yes, I know. Come over now. I haven't got surgery this evening so… Yes, OK. I'll be waiting.'

Patricia tried to quell the emotional pangs she felt as she listened to Adam speaking to his ex-wife in that amicable way. Shouldn't he be slightly acerbic when he spoke to the woman who'd sabotaged his marriage?

'That was Lauren,' he said unnecessarily. 'Tony is giving her a hard time again so she's bringing Rebecca over for a week while she has a break from him.'

'Are they both going to stay with you?' The all-important question was out before she could check herself.

'Rebecca will stay, but Lauren's booked herself into a health farm. She's kept phoning me about Tony's unreasonable behaviour so I've made contingency plans for when they split up which Lauren is sure will happen permanently before long.'

'So what are the plans you've made?' she asked quietly.

Adam's eyes were questioning. Maybe he was sensing her mixed emotions about the way he was accommodating this difficult ex-wife.

'I'm simply doing this for Rebecca's sake. They have a full-time, live-in nanny who will look after the twins, but Lauren tells me she doesn't want to leave Rebecca in the house with Tony. I don't think Rebecca was exaggerating when she said that Tony didn't like her.'

Patricia shivered. 'Poor little lamb!'

She felt a rush of pity for Adam's dear little daughter. She'd taken to her almost as if she were her own child.

She looked down at her own beautiful daughter who was rubbing her eyes as she woke up, her little lips quivering into a smile. She would make sure that she never inflicted an unfeeling stepfather on her own child. She would guard her independence.

Adam put a finger out to touch Emma's hand. She gurgled happily and reached out her arms towards him. Patricia swallowed hard. Adam would make the perfect stepfather but she had to stop wishing for the moon and be practical.

This was an idyllic state of noncommitment they were both enjoying at the present moment, divorced from the realities of real life. As long as she didn't allow her heart to rule her head she wouldn't dream up such an impossible, impracticable situation. She'd made one bad error of judgement in believing that Ben had been the man she'd wanted in her life. She was on the rebound now, vulnerable and still desperately unsure of her own emotions.

Was she capable of having a light-hearted affair with a man who was raising such deep seated emotions in her, making her conjure up dreams for the future that couldn't possibly become a part of reality?

CHAPTER FIVE

'IT'S good to see you looking so well, Mrs Sutton,' Patricia said, as she reached for the sphygmomanometer. 'I'm just going to take your blood pressure. I need to keep a check on this now that we've put you on HRT.'

She pumped up the cuff she'd fastened around her patient's arm before listening to the diastolic and systolic heartbeats of her patient as she watched the column of mercury falling on the sphygmomanometer.

'Good. Your blood pressure hasn't changed since we started you on your medication after your heel bone scan back in April.'

'Will my osteoporosis get worse, Dr Drayton?' Catherine Sutton asked tentatively. 'You explained everything to me after my appointment with the specialist, but I still worry.'

'You are still at risk of further fractures if you don't take care so you need to be doing all the right things. You've joined the Osteoporosis Society like we talked about, haven't you?'

'Oh, yes. They've been really helpful. They sent me booklets on how to improve my health. I'm eating loads more spinach, broccoli and other green vegetables, drinking lots of milk and walking as much as I can to strengthen my bones.'

Patricia smiled. 'Good! That's what we like to hear. Mr Fairburn, your specialist, wrote to me to say he thought you should be on HRT and Fosimax. Are you happy about that?'

Mrs Sutton pulled a wry face. 'I don't like the Fosimax very much. I have to take it first thing on an empty stomach and then I can't have anything to eat or drink for at least half an hour. I'm absolutely gasping for my first cup of tea, I can tell you!'

Patricia smiled. 'I can imagine. But it's worth following the instructions. Fosimax can help to slow down the loss of bone density and in some cases it can actually increase bone density.'

She leaned across towards her patient. 'How's your wrist now? I haven't examined it since you last came to see me.'

Mrs Sutton wriggled her fingers to show their increased mobility. 'It's fine, Doctor. I had the plaster off in May and I've been going to physiotherapy at the hospital.'

As she watched her patient roll down her sleeve at the end of the examination, Patricia thought how quickly the months were passing by. The month of June was already upon them. The summer was flying past and her relationship with Adam was still in a state of flux. She was still trying to keep a realistic view of how she hoped their relationship would develop, but since Adam had been having more contact with his ex-wife, things hadn't been easy. It was as if their relationship had been put on hold.

She dragged her thoughts back to her professional situation as she smiled encouragingly at her patient who was standing up and holding out her hand towards her.

'You've all been so good to me, Doctor,' Catherine Sutton said. 'I always know I can come and have a chat with you if I get depressed. I never thought I would end up with osteoporosis when I was in my fifties.'

'Come and see us any time, Mrs Sutton,' Patricia said.

'But there's really no need to get depressed. You're a model patient and you're going to improve if you carry on like this.'

Her patient smiled. 'I hope so. Goodbye, Doctor.'

Patricia closed the door after her patient and went back to the desk. Glancing at her list on the computer, she saw that no more patients had been added during the course of the morning. She switched off the computer and leaned back in her chair. From the consulting room next door she could hear the faint hum of voices, although the actual words were indistinguishable. Adam's deep voice mingled with that of a higher-pitched female one.

Since their picnic by the river there hadn't been much contact between them. She felt irritated by the fact that Lauren was claiming so much of Adam's time. She'd never actually met Adam's ex-wife but she'd found her resentment growing. After Lauren had left Rebecca with Adam and spent a week at a health farm, she'd asked him to keep Rebecca until she sorted herself out. Apparently, the situation in the Crawford household wasn't getting any easier.

But looking after Rebecca had meant that Adam had been obliged to make extra domestic arrangements. Over coffee at the practice one morning he'd explained how he was coping.

Apparently, he was now employing Penny, the daughter of Vera, his cleaning lady. Penny was a young mother who'd been a nurse before her own baby had arrived, and she was only too happy to help out with caring for Rebecca, especially as Adam had agreed she should bring her own baby with her. She'd been struggling to keep up the payments on her little car so the wages and generous travel allowance Adam paid her were very welcome. Her part-time job entailed collecting Rebecca from the school she attended in Moortown and looking after her when Adam was on duty.

But the main difference in domestic arrangements at Adam's house was the numerous visits by his ex-wife. Some evenings and most weekends Lauren came over to see her daughter, and Patricia had made a point of staying away.

Not that she'd been invited! That rankled. Patricia couldn't help wondering if Adam was still holding a torch for this woman whom he'd once described to her as being beautiful and talented.

She leaned back in her chair and gave a deep sigh as she reviewed the unsatisfactory situation. Was she feeling just the tiniest bit jealous? She told herself she had no right to be jealous. Adam was a good father and he was only doing what was best for Rebecca?

Her face flushed guiltily as she heard the sound of someone tapping on her door. Adam was in the room before she had time to compose herself. It was a good thing he couldn't read her thoughts at that moment!

'We've got to get this water situation at the holiday village sorted,' he said, his face stern. 'I've just had another holidaymaker in, complaining of diarrhoea.'

Patricia quickly adopted a professional manner. She'd never seen Adam looking so put out about a medical problem before.

'Richard said he spoke to Tony Crawford, the owner of the holiday village, when we had the last outbreak of gastrointestinal problems. He was assured that checks had been made and the water supply was safe, but Richard has advised his patients to boil their water or buy bottled drinking water until we get to the root of it all.'

Adam sank into the patient's chair opposite Patricia. 'You know what this boils down to—pardon the pun— don't you? Money! That money-grabbing idiot who built that so-called holiday village has been cutting corners and putting the health of our patients at risk. You know who he is, don't you?'

'Tony Crawford is Lauren's husband, isn't he?' she said evenly.

'Soon to be ex-husband, if what Lauren says is true,' he said vehemently. 'One thing's for sure, I'm not going to let him near my daughter again. Lauren told me she's planning to divorce him as soon as she's sorted out the financial side with her solicitor. Anyway, to return to the water situation. Will you come down there with me this afternoon? I've phoned him and he's agreed to be in his office on the site. To be honest, I don't trust myself to deal with him in a professional way. I'm too personally involved with the wretched man. I think you would be a calming influence.'

He was leaning forward, his eyes flashing with annoyance as he spoke.

'I expect I could be a calming influence,' she said. 'I'll give Helen a ring and see if she'll keep Emma with her this afternoon. I don't think she's got anything planned for today. But you'll have to try and be a bit more objective about this and ignore the fact that he's upsetting Lauren and Rebecca. Maybe we should hand the whole problem over to the environmental health people.'

'I've already spoken to them,' Adam said, his voice ominously quiet. 'They said they would look into the problem but a mild attack of diarrhoea among holiday-makers wasn't top on their list of priorities. Apparently, many of the holidaymakers have been trying to drink the village pub dry and they thought that might be one of the contributory factors. So I think we should speed things up. Well, there's no harm in checking it out ourselves, is there?'

She watched his stern expression change as he leaned back and relaxed, a reluctant smile appearing on his lips.

'OK, you're right, Patricia! I wouldn't be getting so hopping mad if I didn't hate the man! But he's made my daughter's life a misery. As far as I know, he's never actually caused her any physical harm but the drip, drip, drip of unkind remarks has undermined her confidence. She's only a little five-year-old and—' He broke off as his voice became more charged with emotion.

'The joys of being a single parent!' he said, in a more light-hearted tone. 'At least that's what it feel like most of the time, with Lauren swanning around and dropping in for a few hours when it suits her.'

Adam moved towards Patricia, placing a finger under her chin to tilt her face so that she had to look up into his eyes. 'I've missed having time to be with you when I'm off duty.'

She suppressed a shiver as she heard the husky emotion in his voice. Looking up into his eyes, she saw that expression of tenderness that always made her go weak at the knees.

'I've missed you, too, but there's no reason why I shouldn't come over to see you when you're looking after Rebecca.'

'It's not as easy as it sounds,' Adam said carefully. 'When Lauren drops in—and I can never be sure when that will be—all hell can be let loose! One minute she's as sweet as pie and the next she's ranting on about Tony. It upsets Rebecca and I'm left to comfort her after

Lauren's gone and…' He raised his hands towards the ceiling.

'I'm doing all this for the sake of my daughter, but I've got my own life to lead, so if you're prepared to take your chance amid the mayhem, please, please, come and see us!'

'I didn't think you needed me,' Patricia said quietly. 'And I hadn't realised you were going through a rough time with Lauren. I know you told me that Penny seems to be efficiently looking after her before you get home so…'

'That's exactly it,' he said softly, reaching forward to take both her hands in his. 'Penny is efficient, and I'm grateful for that. But efficiency isn't all that Rebecca needs at the moment. Between Lauren and Rebecca I feel emotionally drained. And, like I said a moment ago, I miss you so much.'

'You only had to ask,' she said, revelling in the feel of his fingers clasped around hers. Her body ached for contact with him. Just being near him wasn't enough. 'I'd be happy to help.'

'And there was something else,' Adam said. 'I remember when we had our picnic by the river, you told me that after all you'd suffered with Ben, you weren't ready for another relationship. I reckoned that by holding off for a few weeks, it might give you more time for your wounds to heal.'

Patricia looked up into his eyes. 'I think the wounds are healing nicely. I'm feeling much stronger, Doctor.'

His handsome face lit up as he smiled. 'I'm glad to hear it. Are you feeling strong enough to come out to the house for the weekend and help me do battle with whatever family crisis presents itself? I wouldn't want you to suffer a setback.'

She smiled back at him. 'I think I could cope if my personal physician was in attendance.'

'I'm sure that could be arranged,' he said solemnly.

Gently, he brought his lips down over hers. She savoured the delicious, exciting moment, with its promise of the weekend ahead.

'But what about Lauren?' Patricia asked as she pulled herself away, remembering that they were still in the surgery. 'Won't she want to have Rebecca to herself?'

He laughed. 'Lauren is not over-endowed with maternal instinct. She'll be only too happy to lie on a sun lounger, topping up her tan, and let everybody else take charge of the child-care. And she never stays very long. After she's spent the dutiful couple of hours she goes off to a hotel. I have a feeling there might be a new boyfriend in the offing.'

Patricia felt relieved to hear it! She would definitely try to banish the pangs of jealousy when they next arose.

'Well, it's going to be...er...interesting to meet Lauren.'

'You won't see much of her, I expect. She can be difficult but she won't be there long enough to get on your nerves.'

Patricia wasn't too sure about that but she kept her thoughts to herself! She was trying not to prejudge Adam's ex-wife.

'OK, you're on. Now, what time is our meeting at the holiday village this afternoon?'

Tony Crawford was sitting at a huge desk scattered with papers when his secretary ushered them in.

'Dr Young and Dr Drayton to see you, Tony.'

As he hauled himself to his feet and came towards her, Patricia could see that here was a man who enjoyed good living to excess, a man who obviously had never heard of moderation. He was grossly overweight but the cut of the expensive suit helped to disguise this to a certain extent. His round, fleshy face broke into a smile as he held out his hand to her.

She felt alarmed as she heard the wheezing of his chest and noted the breathlessness that the simple act of standing up and walking across the room had engendered.

'Nice to meet you, Dr Drayton, or may I call you Pat?' he wheezed, pausing to catch his breath before continuing, 'I did my homework, you see—looked you up on the internet. You can call me Tony. Everybody does.'

He held out a large hand towards her and she noticed the swollen fingers. His circulation was obviously very sluggish. In spite of her antipathy towards him, her professional self was hoping that he was under the care of a good cardiologist. But looking at the poor state of his health now, she very much doubted whether he was doing anything at all to take care of his heart. He was the type of man who wouldn't take kindly to being told how to look after himself.

She noticed that he was glancing nervously towards Adam as he talked. Now he turned slightly and nodded at him.

'How're you doing, Adam?'

'Let's get down to business, Tony,' Adam said, moving towards the desk. He held out a chair towards Patricia. 'Come and join me here.'

Tony moved slowly back to his place behind the desk, sinking down onto the enormous leather chair with a loud sigh of obvious relief. Pressing a switch, he buzzed his secretary who appeared within seconds.

'What's it to be, folks? Tea, coffee or a proper drink?'

They both asked for coffee. Tony ordered a whisky. Adam was tapping his fingers impatiently on the side of the desk.

'I've had a couple more patients with diarrhoea,' he began quickly. 'I'm going to get the health authority to do a thorough check on your water supply.'

The genial air of their host vanished as he banged his pudgy fist down on the table, causing a dish of paper clips to rattle alarmingly.

'There's nothing wrong with my water supply. I installed the very best pipes. That other doctor who came a couple of months ago was satisfied with—'

He broke off, scowling, as the secretary appeared with a tray of coffee cups and a large glass of whisky.

'Put that tray on the table over there, will you, Deirdre? We'll drink later… Now, as I was saying, the water supply—'

'Excuse me, Tony,' the secretary interrupted tentatively. 'I've been wondering if the problem could be with the spring water. I've lived round here since I was a child and there have been problems with it over the years. I remember once when they found a dead sheep in the stream up the hill—'

'What stream?' Adam snapped.

'Just leave the tray, Deirdre,' Tony said, his voice ominously quiet. 'You're not paid to wonder about things that don't concern you. Just let me get on with—'

Adam stood up. 'Come and sit over here, Deirdre, and tell us more about this stream and the spring water.'

He towered above the chair, as if defending the nervous secretary from her obviously irate boss. Tony's large face had grown a fiery red as he seethed with anger at this untimely interruption. For a few moments he clutched his chest and grimaced

'This damned indigestion,' he muttered, pulling a packet of indigestion tablets from his pocket and putting a couple in his mouth. 'Blooming nuisance! Pass me that whisky, Deirdre.'

The secretary jumped to her feet and held out the glass towards her boss who took a large gulp.

Adam leaned forward towards him, his professional self coming to the fore. 'Are you sure it's indigestion you're suffering from? Have you seen a doctor about it?'

'Huh! Doctors! I'm seeing two doctors now, aren't I?' He gave a grotesque laugh. 'Haven't seen a doctor since the last one told me to lay off the booze. The trouble with doctors is they want to interfere with the way you run your life, and I'm not standing for that. Indigestion never killed anybody.'

'Have you had a check on your heart recently?' Patricia asked.

'There's nothing wrong with my heart! You're as bad as the rest of them.'

Adam shook his head. 'We can only advise you, but if you're not going to listen we may as well get on with the business in hand. What were you saying about the spring water, Deirdre?'

The secretary had started fiddling with one of the pens at the edge of the desk, her eyes firmly fixed away from her boss.

'Well, you see, when we first started using the spring water I had my doubts because—' She broke off as she glanced towards Tony.

Patricia leaned towards her encouragingly. 'Is it the spring that forms the stream that flows down the hill near the white house? It passes through old Mr Jenkins's farm, doesn't it?'

Deirdre nodded. 'You used to live round here, didn't you, Dr Drayton?'

Patricia nodded. 'When I was a child I used to play in the stream with my sister. All the children did. By the time it had flown through Mr Jenkins's farmyard, past his manure heap and down to the bottom of the hill it was completly unfit to drink. None of the locals would touch it, but often the visitors picnicking by the stream would fill their plastic mugs with it. Many years ago it was rumoured to be pure water and very good for you, but not any more.'

All the time she'd been speaking she'd kept her eyes fixed on the hapless Tony. Patricia was relieved to see that he was no longer rubbing his chest so the pains must have subsided. She watched as his expression changed from anger to apprehension.

'You haven't been conning the poor holidaymakers with outdated fables, have you, Tony?' Adam asked evenly.

For a moment, Patricia felt almost sorry for the man as he covered his face with his hands. But almost instantaneously he recovered his composure and his characteristic air of bravado returned.

'It was a gimmick to please the tourists,' he said, in a loud, truculent tone. 'Anybody would have gone along with it. People on holiday love the local folklore. I was about to start having the stuff bottled. We've got our own label and—'

'There was a new delivery of bottles and labels just arrived, Tony,' the secretary began in a conciliatory tone, obviously hoping she hadn't spoken out of turn and risked her job. 'Shall I—?'

'I think you've done enough for one day, Deirdre,'

her boss said in an acerbic tone. 'Just go and get on with those letters I asked you to finish.'

Deirdre scuttled out, glancing only at Patricia who was smiling encouragingly.

'Don't worry, Deirdre,' she said. 'Tony can't sack you for telling the truth—that's if you still want to work here.'

'Your job's safe, Deirdre,' Tony called after her in a resigned tone. 'But just keep your mouth shut till I've got this sorted. We don't want the local press descending on us. Bad for trade and you'd have no job to come to.'

He turned hostile eyes on Adam as the door closed behind his secretary. 'All I was trying to do was earn a few extra quid. Is that such a crime? I didn't know all this about the stream being polluted. I went up to see the old boy who owns it when I first heard about there being some sort of special water running by the—'

'Sam Jenkins doesn't own the stream,' Patricia put in quickly. 'What made you think—?'

'Well, one of the local labourers—the man who first told me this fairy story about this special water—said he did. He told me to go up and have a chat with the old boy and see if we couldn't work something out to convince the tourists it was good stuff to drink.'

'Rip off the tourists, you mean?' Adam said dryly.

Tony grinned. 'Anything to keep them happy and separate them from their money at the same time. When I saw old man Jenkins he was all for it. Mind you, he didn't give me permission for free. I never for one moment believed he owned the stream but I knew it would keep him quiet if I gave him a bit of pocket money now and again.'

Patricia stood up and walked over to the window, looking out beyond the chalets and cottages towards the hill where she'd lived as a child. The white house was obscured by trees at this angle but she could just make out Sam Jenkins's farm near the top of the hill.

'He's an old rogue,' she said softly. 'Always an eye to the main chance.'

'Sounds a bit like you, Tony,' Adam said. 'I bet the two of you got on well.'

'Now, listen here, Dr High and Mighty, I've had to work hard for every penny I've earned. You with your fancy education! I wasn't born with a silver spoon in my mouth. I spent my childhood in a children's home and—'

'So did I, as it happens,' Adam said quietly.

The room seemed very quiet as Patricia moved swiftly back to the desk. She could feel the tension between the two men, eyeing each other as if they were sparring partners in a fight.

For a few seconds Tony seemed lost for words. When he found his voice he spoke slowly and hesitantly. 'Lauren never told me you—'

'I never told Lauren. It wasn't something she would have wanted to know about.'

Adam leaned back in his chair. 'My parents were very poor. They split up when I was two. My mum had a boyfriend who took her off to live in Germany. Dad went to Australia. Neither of them wanted me so I was put in a home. I stayed there until I went off to medical school.'

Tony whistled. 'Well, I'll be blowed! And I had you marked down as a real toff. So how come you've got the big posh house? You don't get that on a doctor's salary.'

Adam ran a hand through his dark hair as he stood up and began to pace the room impatiently.

'I'll give you the shortened version, if you really must know. My dad went into the import-export business out in Australia and made a bit of money. I had no idea I was his sole beneficiary.' He frowned. 'In fact, over the years, having heard nothing from him, I wondered sometimes if he'd died. But he was just a shadowy figure who'd abandoned me so I felt nothing for him.'

As he leaned against the window-sill, breathing deeply, Patricia could see that talking about his background was emotionally draining to him.

'A few months after my divorce from Lauren I got this letter from a solicitor in Australia. They said they'd had trouble tracking me down. Apparently, my dad had died, leaving everything to me. He'd written me a letter, the only contact I'd ever had with him from the time he left me when I was two and—'

He broke off, as if realising that he was divulging more than he'd meant to. Looking across the room at Tony, he said, 'So does that answer your question?'

'Certainly does!'

Patricia noticed the admiration in Tony's expression as he began speaking again.

'So you had a poor start in life but now you've hit the jackpot. Poor Lauren! I reckon she wouldn't have let you divorce her so easily if she'd known you were going to come into a fortune.'

'Hardly a fortune, but it's been a great help.' Adam was already making for the door. 'Look, we've got to go.' His tone became brisk and professional. 'So long as you agree to suspend your spring water venture completely, Tony, we won't take this any further. OK?'

Tony heaved himself out of his chair and crossed the room to grab Adam by the hand. 'You have my word, Adam.'

Adam raised an eyebrow as he shook Tony's hand.

Tony gave a wry laugh that set him off coughing again. 'I know what you're thinking,' he gasped between bouts. 'Can you trust me?'

'You'll be the one who suffers if I can't,' Adam said evenly. 'I'll give you two days to suspend activities, after which I'll start—'

'Don't worry. Now that I know what kind of man you really are, Adam…' Tony broke off. 'By the way, does Lauren know you came into some money?'

'No, but I expect you'll tell her.'

'Not if you don't want me to.'

'Makes no difference to me, Tony,' Adam said dryly. 'She's your wife.'

'Ah…but I don't think she's going to stay much longer. Keeps threatening to leave me, and she's always off gallivanting somewhere or other. Well, you know what she's like, don't you?'

Adam gave a wry smile. 'Don't I just! As far as telling her my dad left me some money, it's not important one way or the other. I've always supported my daughter financially and made provision for her education. Rebecca will want for nothing.'

Patricia felt relieved that the two men were for the moment in complete accord.

'And how's my little Rebecca?' Tony asked, in a subdued tone. 'I was surprised when Lauren told me you'd insisted she live with you for a while.'

Adam's eyes flickered but he didn't contradict Tony's misconception. If that was what Lauren wanted Tony to believe there was no point in setting the record straight.

'Do you really care how Rebecca is?' he asked in a carefully controlled voice.

The truculent attitude returned. 'Look, mate, I know

we had our differences, me and Rebecca, but that child would try the patience of a saint. Her mother's always spoiled her rotten and I've got my own boys to look after. If they have to take second place to a spoiled little brat who—'

Adam took a step forward and Patricia noticed that he was clenching and unclenching his fists, as if trying to control the physical violence that was welling up inside him as he defended his daughter.

'Was that why you shook her till she screamed for Lauren to come and take her away?'

His voice was ominously quiet, but Patricia could see his patience was wearing very thin. She moved to his side and put her hand on his arm. He was breathing heavily and she could feel tremors of emotion coursing through his strong, athletic body. Tony was much the heavier of these two men, but Adam, in the peak of fitness, could have felled him with a raised hand.

Tony scowled. 'Is that the sort of lie that Lauren's spreading about me?'

'No, that's what my little five-year-old daughter told me when I was reading her a bedtime story about a wicked stepmother,' Adam said evenly.

Tony pursed his lips. 'Well, she needed a good telling-off. My old dad would have taken the belt to me for being cheeky like she was.'

Patricia shivered. 'Perhaps it's just as well Rebecca is staying with Adam,' she said in a conciliatory tone. She took firm hold of Adam's arm before a further confrontation could evolve. 'Come on, let's go,' she said quietly.

Tony was watching them through the window as they drove away. Patricia breathed a sigh of relief as the car turned the corner.

'Phew! That could have been very nasty,' she said,

turning to look at Adam's stern profile, his hands gripping the steering-wheel. 'I wouldn't like to get into a situation where we were really at loggerheads with Tony. Best to keep on the right side of him, I should think.'

Adam's expression relaxed. 'I think Tony and Lauren deserve each other.'

Patricia laughed. She was feeling more secure about Adam's ex-wife now. The more he showed that his feelings for Lauren were cold the more she liked it.

'I surprised him when I told him about my background, didn't I?' Adam said lightly, as he steered the car along Highdale main street.

'You surprised me as well,' Patricia said. 'I'd no idea you'd had that sort of...difficult upbringing.' She hesitated before plunging straight in. 'Was it hard for you to get into medical school?'

He stopped the car in front of Patricia's house and looked pensively through the windscreen. A wasp had settled on the windscreen wipers and Patricia watched its pathetic efforts to crawl up the slippery surface as she waited for Adam's reply. It seemed a long time coming. Just when she was beginning to think she'd definitely overstepped the mark this time she heard his quiet, carefully thought-out response.

'Let's say it wasn't easy. I suppose I had to work a bit harder than someone from a family home where the parents are one hundred per cent behind you. Anyway, it was a dream I had ever since I had a spell in hospital with a broken leg when I was a child and I admired all these efficient people in white coats who went about making people feel better. It seemed like such an interesting and worthwhile profession.'

Her hand was on the doorhandle. 'Would you like to

come and have a cold drink in my back yard before I go and get Emma?'

He smiled. 'I most certainly would. All that sparring and beating about the bush has made me thirsty.'

In the kitchen Patricia switched on her new electric juicer and prepared a jug of freshly squeezed orange juice. Carrying it through into the small back garden, she laid it on her new pine table.

'Just big enough for two, my garden,' she said, easing herself into the chair beside the high stone wall. 'Thanks very much for sending me the terracotta plant pots that your previous owners left behind. If I hadn't known their origin I would say you'd been out and bought them specially.'

Adam grinned. 'Now, why would I do that?'

She laughed. 'The local garden centre people spilled the beans, and someone had forgotten to remove the price tags. Very generous!'

'Well, I must say they look splendid since you planted those lilies in them. It's a nice sheltered garden.'

She laughed. 'Yes, these high walls keep the wind out. That's the beauty of having such a small space to keep warm. I'm planning to make a small sand pit for Emma next spring.'

She stood up and moved over to the far corner of the tiny garden. 'I thought I could put it just about here.' Patricia pointed to the space she'd earmarked for her project. 'What do you think?'

'Too much sun in that corner,' he said, coming up behind her. 'Emma would have to wear a sunhat all the time and—'

'Only in the middle of summer!' she protested. 'This is Yorkshire.'

Adam swung her round to face him. 'I love it when

you get all indignant! I love the fiery flush that spreads all over your cheeks. In fact...' He stopped, looking down into her eyes with that enigmatic expression that told her he was trying to hold something back.

Oh, if only he'd told her he loved her! But she felt a certain amount of relief that he hadn't because she had no idea how she would handle such a powerful emotion. It would be much safer to stick to a light-hearted romance until her bruised emotions were in a more stable condition.

Looking up, she saw the tender, questioning expression on his face. 'When do you have to collect Emma?' Adam asked huskily.

She hoped she was guessing the reason why he was looking at her like that and it took only seconds for her responding passion to ignite.

'Helen's keeping her till after supper. Brian's got the day off and they're taking all the children to the wildlife park this afternoon.' Patricia paused, before posing the unnecessary question. 'Why?'

He reached forward and pulled her gently into his arms. 'It's so long since we had any time together on our own. I want so much to hold you...'

She responded with an ecstatic shiver to the tender caress of his fingers on her bare arms. The passions she'd been holding back for so long were unleashed as he swept her up into his arms. She was only vaguely aware of her surroundings as he carried her through the kitchen.

'I presume you've got a bedroom somewhere up here,' he whispered as he mounted the stairs.

She tightened her arms around his neck. 'You mean you've never been up here before?'

He gave her a rakish grin. 'Never been invited.'

'Neither has anyone else,' Patricia said laughingly.

'Don't get lost in my enormous house, will you? You'll have to guess which is my room.'

Adam smiled as he carried her through into the larger of the two bedrooms at the top of the narrow staircase.

'I bet it's this one.'

'Right first time. However did you guess?'

'You've only got one teddy bear in here, whereas the other room is piled high with wildlife. So, do I get to claim the major prize?' he whispered huskily, his hands impatiently tugging at the buttons on her cotton blouse.

Afterwards, Patricia couldn't remember how she became undressed. She just knew that in the frenzy and mounting excitement they were both very quickly naked on her bed, enjoying the wildest, most intensely satisfying experience she'd ever known. As Adam brought her to an ecstatic climax she cried out with all the pent-up frustration that had been held back inside her.

But even as she lay back in the crook of his arm Patricia knew that this first torrid encounter wasn't going to satisfy either of them. She could feel the hardness of his manhood against her almost immediately and she moaned with desire as he began to stimulate her heightened senses once more. She felt as if her body were melting, turning into a maelstrom of sensation that demanded more…and more…and more…until she felt the waves of fulfilment crashing over her sated body again…

She became aware that somewhere in this heavenly cloud where she was floating above the earth there was an incongruous sound which didn't fit in with the new ethereal being into which she'd evolved. She hoped the ugly sound would go away and leave her to enjoy her new-found bliss.

'Someone's knocking on the door, Patricia,' Adam said, his hands gently caressing her awake.

She came down to earth with a bang as reality claimed her once again. She made to spring out of bed but Adam's hand detained her.

'I'll go,' he said firmly. 'Take your time.'

His lips were smiling, those sensual lips that had kissed their way into every fibre of her being. She shivered at the memory of their passion.

'Don't go like that.' She giggled.

As he towered above the bed, naked, she admired his muscular frame. He reminded Patricia of one of those pictures of a Greek god she'd had in her picture book as a child, all sinewy muscles, ready to slay the dragon and fight the demons of the underworld or something equally macho.

He adopted a wounded, innocent expression. 'Why ever not? I'm sure your sister will have seen a naked man before, won't she?'

At the mention of her sister she sat bolt upright, clutching the sheet over her naked breasts. 'You're right! It could be Helen bringing Emma back early.'

'It's not early. It's seven o'clock!'

She was relieved to see Adam pulling on the trousers of his suit and fastening the buttons of his crumpled shirt.

'Can't be so late!' She glanced at the clock. Where had the afternoon gone to?

Patricia lay back against the pillows, unwilling to return to the real world. The afternoon had flown past in a haze of sensual pleasure, the most heavenly, blissful afternoon she'd ever spent.

The sound of her sister's voice below in the kitchen galvanised her into action. Jeans, polo shirt, quick comb through the tousled hair and she would be good as new...

'Sorry to disturb you,' her sister said in an amused voice as Patricia padded on bare feet into the kitchen. 'Our babysitter has just arrived at home. Brian and I are going out for a meal so I had to bring Emma back.'

'I hadn't realised it was so late,' Patricia said. 'Thanks ever so much for having Emma.'

'She's been as good as gold.'

Emma held out her arms towards Adam, smiling her toothy grin and babbling excitedly.

'Well, it looks as if you two have met before,' Helen said with a knowing glance at Patricia, as Adam took Emma from Helen.

'Yes, we're old friends,' Adam said, smiling. 'In fact, I was the first man she saw on the day she was born.'

'I heard about that,' Helen's husband Brian said.

A quiet, self-effacing teacher at the local primary school, he usually didn't volunteer much information. But Patricia could see that he certainly seemed to approve of Adam.

'Perhaps you two would like to come with us for a meal,' he continued. 'We could take Emma back home and our babysitter could look after all three of them.'

'That's very kind of you,' Adam said quickly, 'but I've got a million things to do this evening. For a start, I've got to get back to relieve the lady who's looking after my own daughter.'

'You have a daughter?' Helen said, surprised. 'Patricia didn't tell me. How old is she?'

'Five. I'm looking after her for a while until my ex-wife sorts out her present marriage problems.'

Helen stood up. 'Sounds complicated.'

Adam shrugged. 'It is! But that's life, isn't it? Just

when you think you've got it sorted, something— Well, it's been great meeting you…'

As they stood at the door, waving goodbye, Emma tightly curled up against Adam's chest, Patricia allowed herself the wicked luxury of imagining they were a real family—mother, father, baby. Except this father was going home to his own child and maybe his wife—well, ex-wife—and this mother would be left to cope all on her own again.

'I'd better get you in the bath, poppet,' she said briskly, reaching to take Emma from Adam.

The soft baby smell enveloped her. Her child's love was the only thing she could be sure about. That was the only constant emotion that would last for ever when all the other events of her unpredictable future life had taken place.

'Don't forget you're coming for the weekend,' Adam said, dashing upstairs to retrieve his suit jacket.

How could she forget? 'It's already in the social diary,' she said jokingly, although she doubted whether even Adam knew how desolate her diary looked. Normally she would be rushed off her feet with her medical commitments until the end of the week, then the big lull would descend upon her. Saturday and Sunday would stretch ahead in an orgy of washing, ironing, cleaning and shopping.

But not this weekend. Oh, no, she was going to live it up in Adam's beautiful house and let her hair down. She wasn't even going to think about the future…or was she?

CHAPTER SIX

LAUREN was exactly how Patricia had imagined from Adam's first description of her. Tall…much taller than she was, of course, but wasn't everybody? Statuesque almost. Beautiful, well groomed, shining long blonde hair falling to her shoulders, flawless make-up. Only the hard expression on her otherwise attractive features detracted from Patricia's impression that she was looking at a beauty queen or a model who'd just stepped off the catwalk.

As she walked down the stone steps that led from the front porch of Adam's house, her impeccably manicured hands stretched out in greeting, Patricia almost gasped at the apparition. Adam had told her his ex-wife was good-looking and intelligent, too! She'd been a successful career-woman before she'd married Tony.

But beneath the glossy veneer there was a restless air of dissatisfaction, unhappiness almost, as she grasped Patricia's hot, damp hand with her cool fingers.

Lauren smiled, flashing perfect white teeth. 'I'm so glad to meet you at long last, Patricia. I was beginning to think you were a figment of Adam's imagination. He was always talking about you but you never materialised. And this must be Emma.'

She reached forward towards the baby but Emma frowned, fidgeting on Patricia's hip and clinging to her mother's arm.

'Emma's not in a very good mood. It was too hot in

the car for her,' Patricia said, to excuse her daughter's unsociable behaviour.

'No air-conditioning? You really should—'

Lauren broke off as Adam appeared at the top of the steps holding Rebecca by the hand. The little girl gave a shout of pure joy and ran towards Patricia and Emma.

'Patricia! Daddy said you might be coming, but I didn't know... Where've you been? I wanted to see you!'

'I've missed you, too,' Patricia said, bending down to receive a wet, enthusiastic kiss on the cheek from the excited little girl. 'I love your shorts.'

Rebecca smiled proudly. 'Mummy brought them today.'

Patricia watched as she smiled up at her mother who was looking a little put out by the effusive welcome that her daughter had given her.

'You're obviously a great hit in this household, Patricia,' Lauren said in a dry tone. She turned to look up at her ex-husband, her face breaking out into a flirtatious smile. 'What a lucky man you are! All these females vying for your attention.'

Adam was looking at Patricia. The tender expression on his face as he kept his eyes firmly fixed on her helped to renew her confidence. His ex-wife might be tall, talented and beautiful, but she meant nothing to him any more. As long as she kept telling herself this she would be able to withstand the unreasonable pangs of jealousy that had plagued her all the way here as she'd driven through the hot June afternoon.

Adam held out his arms towards Emma who gurgled and reached her plump little hands upwards.

'Obviously likes men,' Lauren said dismissively.

'She likes my daddy,' Rebecca said. 'Daddy, can she play in the paddling pool with me?'

'You'll have to ask her mummy,' Adam said, looking at Patricia.

'I think she'd love to cool off, but I'll have to stay with her all the time, Rebecca. Paddling pools can be dangerous places for babies.'

'We'll all stay by the pool,' Adam said, striding off with Emma in his arms and Rebecca skipping happily by his side.

The paddling pool had been set up on the lawn at the back of the house. It was one of those hot summer days that made the Yorkshire Dales seem like the ideal holiday place. Patricia stretched out on the grass beside the pool, before stripping her daughter down to her nappy.

'Don't take the nappy off, Patricia,' Lauren intervened quickly. 'I wouldn't want Emma to pollute the pool when Rebecca's in there.'

As Patricia lowered Emma into the pool she was glad she'd decided to wear her shorts and a skimpy top. If she got wet—which was more than likely—it wouldn't matter. Adam, too, she noticed, had gone for the casual look. His light brown shorts and white polo necked shirt made him look younger than usual. She caught her breath as he looked towards her. The expression in his eyes was enigmatic. She wondered if he was looking forward to the evening when they would hopefully have some time alone.

Her daughter was shrieking with delight at the cooling effect of the water and Rebecca, now wearing a new pink bikini, was patting a ball towards her. Another present from her mother, perhaps?

She glanced towards Lauren and saw the restless expression on her face as she stood by the pool. She was wearing a superbly cut black sundress with a side split that displayed one of her long, slim, perfectly suntanned legs.

'You obviously don't need any more help here. I'm going to change and catch up on my tan,' she announced, as she turned and made for the house. 'Be a darling and put a sun lounger over by the summer house, will you, Adam?'

Patricia glanced at Adam and saw the wry smile on his face as he stood up.

'Will you be OK with these two, Patricia?' he asked.

Patricia smiled. 'Rebecca will help me with Emma, won't you, darling?'

Adam fixed the chair at the edge of the garden. 'It's far enough away so that Lauren won't get splash marks on her bikini,' he said dryly, returning to the pool.

Patricia laughed. Her laughter died as she saw the beautiful apparition in a white bikini emerging from the house.

'What a figure!' she said, almost to herself.

'The most expensive figure for miles around!' Adam said quietly, with a wicked grin. 'I don't know how she can afford all the money she pays out to her personal trainer at the health club.'

He reached across the pool and squeezed her hand. As their wet hands meshed together she felt a warm rush of tenderness towards him. She really didn't need to worry about his feelings for Lauren. They'd died when his ex-wife had two-timed him, and he was completely over her.

Just as her own feelings for Ben had died when she'd discovered she hadn't been able to trust him any more. They'd both been betrayed. So how could she be sure that either of them was ready for a new romance?

The more time she spent with Adam, the more confused she was becoming. She wanted to be with him every available moment. But how long could it last? Shouldn't it take longer than this before the heart was ready to experience true romantic feelings?

First time around was hard enough but second time around was a maze of unknown possibilities, not least the feeling that when she'd been once bitten shouldn't she be twice shy?

Patricia splashed water over her daughter's back to cool her down. She'd smoothed some sunscreen over her but it would need a re-application soon. Catching sight of Adam looking at her with that heart-rending expression in his eyes that made her go weak at the knees, she told herself to stop being pessimistic about their relationship. She'd promised herself she was going to go with the flow this weekend and not keep looking into the unknown future.

It was almost suppertime before Lauren stirred from her sun lounger and disappeared into the downstairs shower room that led off the kitchen. Patricia noticed she was carrying a garment bag, a vanity case and a sports holdall. Fixing Emma into the well-padded high chair at the head of the kitchen table, she glanced at Adam.

'How many are we going to be for supper?'

He lifted Rebecca onto her two-cushioned chair beside Emma. 'Children's supper now and later there'll just be the two of us.'

'Is Mummy going back to Tony tonight?' Rebecca asked, her innocent blue eyes fixed on her father.

'I expect so, darling,' Adam said, without batting an eyelid.

When Lauren eventually emerged from the shower

room, Patricia could see why it had taken her so long. The impeccable cream linen suit moulded itself to her perfectly formed figure. The strappy high-heeled sandals made her look almost as tall as Adam. Patricia felt like a dwarf in comparison as she spooned the last of the puréed banana into Emma's gooey mouth. She rinsed a baby cloth under the kitchen tap and wiped Emma's face.

'You look great, Lauren,' she said, making an attempt to be friendly

It wasn't easy when you'd spent the afternoon super-vising the paddling pool while the goddess had idled away the time, only moving to renew the suntan lotion on her golden skin!

Lauren ignored her and, smiling a wide, seductive smile, turned her green eyes on Adam. 'I'm going to meet a friend, Adam. The only thing is, I seem to have left my wallet at home, credit cards, cash, cheque book—the lot! So stupid of me, but I wondered if you could help me out.'

Adam's enigmatic expression gave nothing away as he put a hand under his ex-wife's elbow and steered her out of the kitchen.

'We'll discuss the problem in the sitting room,' he said firmly. 'I'll be back in a couple of minutes, Patricia,' he called over his shoulder.

As she lifted the girls down from their chairs, she could hear the low murmur of voices in the room next door growing to a furious crescendo.

'It's not as if you can't afford it!' she heard Lauren say. 'You're not short of money any more, are you?'

'Ah, so that's it! Tony's been talking to you about...'

The rest of Adam's declamation was lost in the hub-bub that was going on in the kitchen as Rebecca started playing her toy trumpet. Just as well, Patricia thought, that she couldn't hear her parents' argument. Adam had obviously hoped to keep it between the two of them.

She piled some bricks in front of Emma who giggled gleefully as she knocked them down with her chubby little hand. Minutes later she heard the front door bang, and Adam appeared in the kitchen.

'Mummy's had to go out,' he said to Rebecca.

She smiled, seemingly not the least bit perturbed by the fact that her mother hadn't said goodbye to her. 'I thought Mummy had come to take me back to Tony. Am I going to stay here another night?'

Adam leaned down and picked his little daughter up. 'You most certainly are!'

'Can I stay here for always?'

He hesitated, looking across at Patricia as if asking for help in answering such a tricky question.

'Always is a long time, Rebecca,' Patricia said, moving over to take hold of the little girl's hands. 'Daddy will have to see what Mummy wants before he can make promises. And sometimes mummies and daddies don't always agree.'

'But you don't shout at Mummy like Tony does, do you, Daddy?' She turned earnest blue eyes up to Adam.

He pulled her closer against him protectively. Caught in the embrace, Patricia could feel the emotion flowing through Adam as he held his small, vulnerable daughter. It was so sad to think that children could be the innocent victims of their parents' quarrels.

'I thought you were going to shout at Mummy just now,' Rebecca said quietly. 'That's why I played my trumpet, so I couldn't hear you. You didn't shout, did you, Daddy? I don't like it when grown-ups shout.'

'No, I didn't shout, darling,' he said quietly, his voice

shaky with emotion. 'Your mummy and I didn't agree on something, but we didn't shout.'

'Good!' Rebecca said. 'Mummy always cries when Tony shouts at her and I don't like to see her cry. All her masky—maska—that black stuff she puts on her eyes starts running and it frightens me. She looks like a witch and she doesn't look pretty like Mummy any more.'

Patricia felt sad as she listened to the touching indictment of grown-up behaviour. Whatever happened to her in the future, she would make sure Emma never had to suffer emotionally as this dear little girl had already suffered. And for as long as she knew Rebecca, she would do all she could to protect her from further harm.

'Who's going to help me put Emma in the bath?' she asked quickly.

'Me! Me!' Rebecca was already struggling to get down from her father's arms.

Patricia lay back against the pillow, revelling in the warm glow that lingered over her as she recovered from their love-making. Glancing across through the open window, she could see the bright full moon shining into the bedroom.

She eased herself away from Adam's arms, taking care not to waken him. He merely gave a contented sigh and continued his rhythmic breathing. Carefully, she drew the crumpled sheet over his chest. It was a warm night, but his chest was damp with perspiration and she didn't want him to catch cold.

Turning on her side, she realised that she was becoming proprietorial. She was behaving like a wife. Well, she felt like a wife! After they'd put their children to bed, they'd made their way upstairs without any discus sion of the fact that they hadn't had supper. They'd both been so anxious to escape into their private world where only the two of them existed.

There had been no need for words as they'd tumbled onto the huge four-poster bed, reaching out for each other, hastily discarding everything that had prevented them from gaining maximum contact with each other.

Patricia felt an involuntary shiver running through her as she remembered the passion they'd ignited together. Adam's caresses had driven her wild with desire, just touching her, then tantalising her until she'd known she couldn't hold out any longer in her quest for fulfilment. As if by some joint secret signal they'd delayed the moment of fusion as long as was humanly possible so that when their bodies had finally joined together the experience had been out of this world.

Her eyes felt wet with tears as she raised her head once more on the pillow to look down at the slumbering Adam. Yes, she felt just like his wife, and that was something she would have to contend with if she was going to live in the real world. Tonight she'd had a heavenly experience, but tomorrow she would have to come to terms with all that their shared experience implied.

She would have to remember that this was supposed to be just a light hearted affair and try to get things back into proportion. She would have to—

Patricia frowned as she heard the insistent ringing of the bedside phone. Neither of them was on call so it couldn't be anything important. She'd actually switched off her own mobile for the weekend. On the other hand, she'd had to tell Helen where she was spending the night, just in case she called round and became worried about her. Or it could be Lauren. Much as she was coming to dislike the woman, she was, after all, Rebecca's mother.

Adam opened his eyes and reached automatically for the phone which was at his side of the bed.

'Dr Young,' he said, in his groggy, barely awake voice. Years of night calls had made him able to react robot-like to the sound of a night-time phone.

She could hear that his caller was a woman and she glanced enquiringly at him. Briefly, he covered the mouthpiece to whisper that it was Jane. She frowned. What on earth did their colleague want with Adam in the middle of the night? Was there some sort of medical crisis she and Richard couldn't handle?

Adam was looking grave, nodding his head, speaking in a low, urgent voice. 'Actually, Patricia is here at the house,' he was saying. 'I'll put her in the picture and call you back.'

Patricia stared at him as he cut the connection. 'What was all that about? I wish you hadn't said I was here.'

He reached for her and pulled her towards him. 'She'd already phoned your sister. Jane needs your help. It's Craig Watson, our kidney patient. His mother phoned Jane and Richard. He's swallowed some pills and is in a bad state. He won't let her call the ambulance. Says he'll cut his wrists if she does. He wants to see you because you've been looking after him. Nobody else will do.'

Patricia listened, her professional brain taking in the details, all the while trying to remain detached so that she could do what was best for her patient.

'Call Jane back and say I'll drive over to see him now,' she said quickly, moving to release herself from Adam's arms.

For a moment he held her tightly against him. 'I don't

want you to drive over there by yourself in the middle of the night. I'm coming with you. Jane said Richard would drive up here to babysit while we're out, if you agreed.'

She nodded. 'OK.'

As Adam drove along the eerily silent, moonlit lanes that led to the Watsons' house, Patricia felt as if she'd suddenly been transported to a different world. Only a short time ago she'd been cocooned in the seductive warmth of the four-poster, devoid of all worldly worries. But now here she was, trying to get her head round the fact that she would have to confront a difficult suicidal patient.

The tortuous upland road now straightened out. Adam took one hand off the wheel and touched her arm. 'Would you like me to come inside the house with you?'

She nodded. 'I would feel safer if you did, but I don't know how Craig will react. If he says he only wants me to be there it might be safer if you stay in the car.'

'We'll make a decision when we get there,' he said firmly, his fingers tightening on her arm.

He took his hand away as he turned the car down the rough track that led to the Watson house. In the moonlight, Patricia couldn't see over the high stone walls on either side of the narrow track. She felt closed in, unable to escape from an inevitable confrontation. She tried to remember all the things she'd learned about suicidal patients during her training. The main idea was to remain calm. She could do that. The rest would depend on how badly Craig had harmed himself.

'Have you got something to wash out Craig's stomach?' Adam asked quietly.

She patted the medical bag at her feet. 'Yes. And I've

got an emetic to make him vomit. I'll use whichever one is appropriate, depending on his physical state. If he's already unconscious I'll send for the ambulance. I know he's threatened to slit his wrists, but if he's passed out completely he can't do any more harm to himself.'

'And he'd be better off in hospital,' Adam said evenly. 'Look, I'm going to come into the house with you, Patricia, because— No, hear me out,' he insisted as she began to protest. 'A suicidal man isn't someone to take risks with. I don't want you to come to any harm. I only wish it had been me he'd asked for instead of you. You're very…you're very special to me, and if anything happened to you…'

She swallowed the lump in her throat. This was the first time Adam had said something tender to her when they weren't actually making love. And here, in a professional situation, she found it especially comforting.

'If anything happened to you I would be devastated,' he finished, his voice husky with emotion. 'I'll come into the house and wait in the kitchen with Craig's mother.'

He turned off the engine in front of the house. The ramshackle building looked decidedly eerie in the moonlight. He was already running round the front of the car to open the passenger door, taking her bag and carrying it to the house. Mrs Watson opened the door as soon as they arrived. She pushed her dishevelled grey hair out of her eyes and stared at them with frightened eyes.

'Craig's gone absolutely beserk.'

'So he's still conscious?' Adam said.

'Yes, but he's ranting and raving about wanting to die. I've never seen him like this. He's taken my new packet of paracetamol into his bedroom and locked the door. I don't know how many he's actually swallowed. He's locked the door and he's threatening to take all of them.'

'When was that, Mrs Watson?' Patricia asked gently.

'It must be a couple of hours ago, I suppose. Yes, I'd fallen asleep in the chair and I was just going to make myself a cup of tea before going to bed when he woke me up in a right old state. He said he'd already had a lot of pills because he didn't want to live any more.'

Patricia put an arm around Mrs Watson's shoulders as she began to cry.

'Then he started saying he wanted to see you, Dr Drayton. He said you would understand what he was going through. I told him it was the middle of the night and I didn't want to waken you but he insisted. Said he'd got a razor in there and would slit his wrists if I didn't send for you.'

'How long is it since you spoke to him?' Adam asked.

'He hasn't been answering me for a while now. I reckon the pills must be taking effect. Will you go and see what's happening, Dr Drayton?'

Adam held Patricia's hand tightly all the way up the stairs, but she motioned him to leave her as she knocked on Craig's bedroom door.

'Craig? It's Patricia Drayton. Can you open the door?'

There was no sound. Adam, standing beside her, drew in his breath. 'If he's unconscious I'll have to break the door down.'

'Who've you got with you?' Craig called from the other side of the door.

Patricia gave a sigh of relief. If Craig was talking there was still time to save him.

'Dr Young is with me,' Patricia said. 'But I'll come in by myself if that's what you prefer.'

'Only you can come in,' Craig said firmly.

She heard him sliding a bolt and the door was opened a crack. Two bright, frightened eyes were staring at her.

She stepped inside and Craig shot the bolt back into place.

'I want to die,' he said, moving slowly back to the bed. 'That's the only way out of this mess.'

She could see the packet of pills and a large cutthroat razor. It was a real relic from the past. Laid out like that on his bedside table, it looked highly dangerous, but she conquered her fear. She had the distinct impression that Craig's suicide attempt was a cry for help rather than a determined effort to end his life. If Craig had systematically swallowed the whole packet of pills he would have been deeply unconscious by now.

Patricia sat on the edge of Craig's bed and reached for his hand, her fingers moving round to the wrist. He had a full, normal pulse. He couldn't have swallowed many of the pills, if any.

'What's this all about, Craig?' she said, gently. 'You don't really want to die, do you?'

'Yes, I do. Call this living? Hooked up to a rotten machine every night. Saturday night when all my mates are down the pub! I just thought I wouldn't have any more of it.'

Patricia glanced at the dialysis apparatus standing unused beside his bed. 'You won't feel so good in the morning if you don't get your full dialysis tonight.'

'I'm not going to be here in the morning! At least...' Her patient looked up at her, his eyes studying her reaction. 'Do you think when they hear I've tried to commit suicide that I'll get my kidney transplant?'

So that was what Craig was up to! Emotional blackmail! She couldn't help but feel relieved that it definitely wasn't a serious attempt at suicide, but at the same time she had to clarify the situation for her confused patient.

She leaned forward and took hold of his hand. 'Craig,

if you think that attempting suicide will put you to the head of the transplant list you're very much mistaken. It won't make a scrap of difference. When a suitable kidney becomes available you'll get your chance. But if you start giving up now we'll lose everything. Now, you've been very patient so far. Don't spoil everything. Your poor mother is suffering so much by what you're doing tonight.'

His angry expression softened. 'Poor Mum! She doesn't deserve this, I know. But something just snapped tonight. Andy, one of my mates from the football club, called round and said he'd take me down to the Coach and Horses and bring me back. I told him I wasn't supposed to drink like I used to. After he'd gone I felt like a freak. I knew they'd all be talking about me in the pub, saying how pathetic I was, and—'

'Craig, nobody thinks you're pathetic. We all think you're very brave. Now, I'm going to start your dialysis and you're going to lie here and try to get some sleep. How many pills did you take?'

Craig pulled a wry face. 'Just a couple.'

'That won't harm you. Now, let's get you fixed up with this. Just lie still. I'll plug you in...'

She could hear Adam's voice from the other side of the door. 'Is everything all right in there?'

'Fine!' Patricia called, turning back to look at her patient. 'Do you mind if Dr Young comes in?'

Craig gave a resigned shrug. 'He's OK. I don't mind him. It's those hospital people who get on my nerves. Always preaching at me about cleaning the equipment and everything.'

'That's their job, Craig,' she said, as she went over to unbolt the door. 'They're only trying to help you, just like we all are.'

Adam put his hands on her shoulders and held her against him. 'I was worried when everything went quiet,' he whispered.

She allowed herself the comfort of his embrace for a couple of seconds, before breaking away and going back to her patient.

'Craig's only taken a couple of pills,' Patricia said quietly, 'so we're starting up his dialysis for the night.'

Adam had moved swiftly to the bedside table to remove the ancient cutthroat razor. 'Haven't seen one of these since I was at medical school. Where did you get it from?'

'It was my dad's.' Craig hesitated, then took a deep breath before continuing, 'Dad cut his wrists with it and bled to death when I was fifteen. When the police had finished examining it I hid it away in my room. I thought if ever life started getting me down I could go and join my dad. I didn't know what I was in for then, did I?'

Patricia tried to swallow the lump that had risen in her throat. 'Craig, I'm so sorry. I had no idea you'd had to go through an ordeal like that. But, believe me, I understand how you must have felt. My own father commited suicide when I was still a child and it took me a long time to get over it.'

Craig's eyes widened and he leaned forward towards Patricia. 'Really? But you got over it eventually, didn't you?'

She nodded. 'Life is very precious, Craig. We must always make the best of what we've got. I know it's an old cliché, but it's a good idea, when we're feeling down, if we count our blessings and try to put up with the difficult things in our lives.'

Patricia broke off, hoping Craig wouldn't think she was preaching at him and switch off. But from the expression on his face he seemed to be hanging on her every word as if she were giving him a lifeline. Would it now be safe to remind him again about his poor mother and what she was going through?

'You must realise what this is doing to your poor mother,' she said. 'She must be out of her mind with worry, thinking that she might lose another loved one in the same awful way. Won't you let her in to see you now?'

Craig's bitter expression softened. 'OK. She's a good mum, but she doesn't half go on at me all the time. Sometimes I can't stand it. I just want to escape and live my own life again.'

Adam nodded understandingly. 'We all know what you're going through, Craig, but hang in there. You're tough enough to survive all this.'

Craig glanced at him gratefully. 'Do you really think I'm tough, Doctor?'

'I most certainly do! I bet you're pretty good on the football pitch, aren't you?'

'I played for Moortown five years ago!'

'Did you really?' Adam said. 'I haven't played football since I was at medical school and we didn't have a very good team. They would take anybody who could kick a ball about.'

Craig laughed and Patricia felt a warm glow as she watched the two men deep in a conversation that was clearly having a therapeutic effect on their patient.

'We'll see how you get on when you've had your transplant,' Adam was saying. 'You'll need to get strong before you start training, of course, but after that... Anyway, I'm going to get your mum. Now, you'll set her mind at rest, won't you, Craig? You're all she's got...'

* * *

The first glimmer of dawn was shining over the top of the eastern hills as Adam stopped the car in front of the house. Richard came out onto the steps, his face anxious.

'Well?'

'He's going to be OK,' Adam said, leading the way inside. 'How are the girls?'

'Both fast asleep,' Richard said.

Adam moved along the corridor towards the kitchen. 'I'll make some coffee and we'll give you a full report.'

Patricia found it strange to be sitting at the kitchen table with her two medical colleagues in Adam's house, having a medical discussion. The situation was highly irregular that she was staying here at all. She wondered how much Richard was reading into her relationship with Adam. It would soon be common knowledge that she'd spent the night with him.

Would this put added pressure on them to regularise their relationship when neither of them was ready to look further than the present moment? Was this going to signal the end of their idyllic state of limbo and force a decision on commitment or break-up upon them?

At the end of her report on Craig's state of mind, Patricia watched as Richard made a few notes.

'I'll have to make a report on this to the hospital at Moortown. But as it was only a cry for help, we won't need to take it any further,' he said. 'Will you call back and check on Craig and his mother later today, Patricia? I know you're not officially on duty but you seem to have the magic touch with him.'

She smiled. 'Of course I will. I'd planned to make a detour on my way home anyway.'

There was a short silence. Richard put down his coffee-cup. 'It's great to see you two getting on so well,' he said in a careful tone. 'I know that everybody at the practice will be—'

'Please, Richard,' Adam broke in. 'We just want to be left on our own. We've both gone through difficult times and we're still trying to come to terms with our past mistakes. We're both just taking one step at a time.'

'I was hurt badly by Ben,' Patricia said, her eyes on Adam. 'I've got to take it slowly.'

Adam's eyes seemed to mirror her sentiments. 'So the fewer people who interfere, the better,' he said firmly.

Richard stood up. 'Hey, I didn't mean we would all be waiting for the sound of wedding bells. Believe me, Jane and I have been in the same situation where everybody thinks they know what's best for you and you still don't know your own mind. I just wanted you to know that we're pleased you're getting on so well. Just enjoy it while it lasts and if things don't work out, well...' Richard shrugged his shoulders. 'No harm done!' he added, a trifle embarrassed as he made for the door.

Patricia waited in the kitchen as Adam escorted Richard to his car. It was easy for Richard to say that no harm would be done. A great deal of harm would be done if they split up after this blissful interlude.

Her heart would be shattered and she knew it would be impossible to mend it.

CHAPTER SEVEN

THE windscreen wipers hummed busily as Patricia drove along the high moorland road. Peering out onto the water-splashed road ahead, she was thinking that it didn't seem a bit like August. She'd thrown her raincoat onto the back seat of her little car because she knew that old farmer Jenkins kept his farmyard gate securely padlocked and all visitors to the property had to go through a small side gate and paddle through the muddy farmyard.

He was a strange old boy was Sam Jenkins! The tales people told about him were legendary. He kept himself very much to himself but the fractured femur he'd sustained falling off a ladder had forced him to spend a few weeks in Moortown General Hospital, and from all accounts he'd been a very difficult patient.

He still insisted on living alone, and submitted to the ministrations of the district nurse with very bad grace. It was the district nurse who'd begged Patricia to persuade him that he needed some physiotherapy but she knew he wasn't going to take kindly to the idea.

She pulled up in front of the forbidding gate and surveyed the NO ENTRY KEEP OUT sign. Climbing out of the car, she hurriedly threw on her raincoat before settling herself on the edge of the boot to pull on her wellingtons. By the look of that mud she would be lucky if it didn't come over the tops!

She was already wet by the time she eased herself through the side gate and began to plough her way across to the kitchen door. She couldn't help smiling to herself as she waded through the brown, muddy stream that flowed through the farmyard. This was the stream for which Tony Crawford had paid Sam Jenkins rights to use the 'special' water!

Swollen by the rain of the past few days, it was a veritable torrent! Years ago, there had been some attempt to fix stepping stones to keep feet dry in times of wet weather but these had long ago been carried downstream.

There had been very little farming done here during the past few years. She'd heard that an old friend of Sam's called in occasionally to check on the few remaining hens who wandered around, pecking at the ground in a desultory fashion, but apart from that the place looked deserted. Patricia could see a scattering of grain in front of the kitchen door, so old Sam must have been able to gather his strength enough to feed the hens this morning.

She glanced at the spot where the stream skirted the manure heap, noting how murky the water looked. True to his word, Tony had ceased his illegal trading in this doubtful liquid and they hadn't had to take any further steps against him. But she still hadn't had a word with Sam Jenkins about it. Not that he would take any notice of her or anybody else! He was a law unto himself, this old man.

She saw him peering cautiously out through a gap in the tattered kitchen curtains after she had knocked twice on the kitchen door.

'Go away!'

'It's Dr Drayton, from the Highdale Practice, Mr Jenkins,' Patricia said firmly. 'I've come to see how you are. Would you like to unlock the door for me?'

The old man grunted and shuffled his way to unbolt the door. 'You can't stay. I'm having a nap. Didn't sleep a wink last night.'

'I could give you something to help you sleep, Mr Jenkins,' she said gently, easing her way past a variety of machines and appliances that littered the kitchen floor in various states of repair.

'Don't believe in medicines. Make you ill. Never had a day's illness in my life till this leg gave out on me.'

He sank down heavily onto the old sofa and stretched out his leg, encased in thick, woollen trousers towards her, tapping the spot where it hurt the most.

'Let me have a look at it for you.'

She moved her fingers over the area of his thigh that had been affected by the fracture. He was so thin she could feel the metal of the plate that had been inserted along the femur to hold both ends of the bone together.

'Are you eating enough?' she asked.

'What sort of a damn fool question is that? I eat what I want, like I always have done.'

She gave up on that one, knowing it was no good suggesting meals on wheels. Even if he agreed, the ladies who gave up their time to the service wouldn't relish making a long drive up here and negotiating the rushing farmyard stream at the end of it.

But she was determined to insist on physiotherapy. There was an excellent physiotherapy department at Moortown General which would arrange for an experienced physiotherapist to visit Sam Jenkins on a regular basis. The treatment and exercises they could give him would help to improve his muscle tone.

'Your leg isn't going to get better unless you exercise it a bit more,' she said firmly. 'It's no good sitting here all day and expecting it to work properly. Your muscles will waste away. You remember the old saying, use it or lose it?'

No reply. Not even a flicker of expression on the old wrinkled face to indicate that he was even listening.

'So I'm going to arrange for a physiotherapist from the hospital to come and see you once a week. He'll help you to get your leg working again so long as you do what he says.'

Sam Jenkins muttered under his breath, 'A man, is it?' He thought about this for a while.

Patricia waited.

'I don't mind a man coming here. He might give me a hand with some of the heavy work I need to do. But I don't like women fussing about the place, poking their noses into what doesn't concern them. I was glad to see the back of my missus when she walked out on me.'

An idea was forming in her head.

'The physiotherapist is too busy to do anything other than help with your leg, but why don't you get a man to come in each day and help you with the chores? And he could help you cook a bit of dinner while he was here as well. You can't be short of money with all that business you've been taking on. I hear you went into the spring water industry.'

A wicked smile hovered on the old man's lips. 'Some of these townsfolk are so daft it's like taking candy from a baby. I remember once, years ago, I put a sign at the end of the lane saying FRESH DUG POTATOES. The cars used to line up outside my gate of a Sunday afternoon while I went round the back, threw a bit of soil into a bag of spuds from the wholesalers and sold them at three times the price I'd paid.'

'You're an old rogue, Sam Jenkins,' Patricia said. 'Still, I don't think you're going to change, are you?'

The old farmer cackled. 'Live each day as if it was your last, that's my motto. And enjoy yourself while you're here. You're a long time dead.'

'Well, shall I ask in the village to see if there's anybody daft enough to want to work for you?'

'Do what you like, lass... Hang on, yes. It might be a good idea. But tell 'em I won't pay 'em unless they work 'ard.'

Patricia was still smiling as she negotiated a difficult three-point turn and drove back down the lane towards the moorland road. Sam Jenkins was an old rogue but she admired his spirit.

It had stopped raining now. She wondered if there would be chance for a walk this afternoon. Emma could do with some fresh air. She'd been looking a bit peaky since the weather had changed for the worst.

Her thoughts turned inevitably to Adam and those first idyllic weeks at the beginning of the summer when everything had seemed so fresh—including their heady romance! Even though she was sure that Richard hadn't been spreading the news that she and Adam were sleeping together, she could tell that most people regarded them as an item.

And to a certain extent she felt that, instead of drawing them together, this new-found common knowledge was driving them apart. She often caught Adam looking at her as if he didn't know how to behave towards her when they were working together with other colleagues near at hand.

Neither of them referred to the unseen problem of where their relationship was going. When they were alone together and when they made love it was heavenly to retreat into their own private world. But as soon as they returned to the reality of the workaday situation something happened to put a block on their natural emotions.

She sighed as she turned into the small drive of Helen's garden, slamming on the brakes as she almost ran into the back of a large, distinctive, black car parked near her sister's front door. Her heart started to beat its familiar tattoo as she wondered why Adam was calling on Helen.

Helen was smiling broadly as she opened the front door. 'A visitor for you, Patricia.'

'So I see.' She lowered her voice. 'How long has Adam been here?'

'Only a few minutes. He's got another appointment so he wanted to catch you when you came to collect Emma.'

They were walking through into the large farmhouse-type kitchen. Patricia always thought this was the best part of the house. Helen and Brian had got the builders to knock the wall down into the old dining room and it had become the central meeting place for everybody. The warmth from the Aga was welcoming as she walked in.

Adam was down on his knees, building a brick castle for Emma. For once she was fascinated by the process and had resisted the temptation to knock it down. Patricia's heart went out to them. At ten months old, Emma was beginning to change from being a baby to a little girl. She could crawl swiftly round the floor and was already able to pull herself up by the leg of a chair. There was no doubt she would soon be walking.

How she loved it when Adam spent time with her daughter! It was impossible to separate her romantic love for him and her gratitude that he was such a wonderful father figure for Emma.

'Hi!' He was hauling himself up onto his feet. 'Sorry, Emma, you'll have to finish that by yourself. I've got to go as soon as I've spoken to Mummy about something.'

'Did you have time to call in and see Craig when you were out on your rounds?' he asked in his professional voice.

'Yes, I spent a short time with him. Physically he's as well as can be expected but mentally…he's struggling a bit. I wish there was something we could do about that transplant. I think I calmed him down, gave him the strength to hold on a bit longer.'

'I'm sure you did. That's why he keeps asking for you. And you went to see old Mr Jenkins, didn't you? How was he?'

She smiled. 'Cantankerous as ever! I'll get physiotherapy to sort him out. That new athletic looking man should be able to put him through his paces.'

Adam grinned. 'I hear he's pretty tough.'

Patricia laughed. 'He'll need to be.' She waited. 'So…?'

Helen had her back to them as she noisily began to wash up the mugs and plates that had accumulated during the long morning.

'Would you like to come out for a meal this evening? I've provisionally booked a table at the Country House.'

'Wow! I'm impressed. Will they have high chairs?'

'Not tonight,' he said quietly. 'I thought it was about time we went out by ourselves for a change. Rebecca is being taken home after school by one of her little friends for a sleep-over in Moortown.'

Helen turned round quickly, peeling off her plastic gloves and slapping them down on the sink. 'So I've invited Emma to have a sleep-over here, haven't I, darling?'

She bent down and chucked Emma under the chin. Emma replied by grinning widely, showing her new teeth and banging down the remains of the castle.

Adam smiled. 'You can see Emma approves. What does Mummy think?'

The idea was becoming more appealing by the second! What was it Sam Jenkins had just told her? Live each day as if it were your last! For once she was going to go along with this.

Patricia smiled. 'Sounds like I've got it gift-wrapped.'

She watched an expression of relief flit across Adam's face and wondered if her cautious attitude to moving on their relationship had made him tread carefully this time. She reminded herself that they'd both agreed to keep their affair light-hearted, uncommitted and temporary, but the more they were together, the harder this was becoming.

And their family commitments added greater pressure. Adam's ex-wife was still causing him grief. It annoyed Patricia that he'd been helping Lauren out financially for the past few weeks. And she was always popping in to see Rebecca just when they were about to have some time to themselves.

She moved slowly towards Adam and put her hands on his waist. 'Yes, it will be good to get away by ourselves,' she said quietly.

This was the most demonstrative she'd been with him when there was someone else in the room. For a moment she'd forgotten that Helen was still there.

Adam bent his head and kissed the tip of her nose. It was a private gesture he made, usually when they were coping with children, and she loved it. Seemingly devoid of passion, it always sent shivers down her spine and reminded her that before long they would find an opportunity to make love.

His eyes were soft as he looked down at her. 'I'll pick you up about seven.'

She raised one finger and touched his face. 'I'll be ready.'

After he'd gone Patricia tried to get back into working mode as she reached down for her daughter.

Her sister put out her hand. 'Oh, no, you don't! Don't disturb Emma when she's busy. Leave her here and take the afternoon off. I may not be a doctor but I've seen the signs of strain on my little sister's face for some time now. It's time you started looking after yourself as well as your patients. It can't be easy, being a single parent.'

Patricia leaned against the kitchen table. 'Don't make me start on self-pity, Helen. I chose to stay by myself when Ben—'

'Isn't it time you made your peace with Ben?'

She stared at Helen. 'Why should I? He two-timed me, and when he did finally come to see Emma he was an absolute pain. He's made it plain that fatherhood is the last thing he wants, so—'

'You can't go round carrying all this bitterness for ever. Ben may be regretting how he behaved but doesn't know what to do. Make contact with him again. Adam's still in touch with his ex even though she's been an absolute bitch. He seems to cope with it and I think that laying old ghosts to rest...'

'Adam copes too much! Sometimes I think she's trying to get him back.'

There! She'd said it out loud, the awful thought that plagued her when she saw Adam giving Lauren money or being patient when she was acting in a difficult way towards Rebecca.

'Ah! The green-eyed monster! I wondered when you'd admit to it.'

'Well, wouldn't you be jealous if you had to watch that woman, with her fancy clothes, living a life of luxury, mostly courtesy of Adam?'

Helen put a hand on her sister's shoulder. 'That's why I was delighted to help when Adam said he wanted to take you out tonight. You've got to talk together about your own precious relationship and find out where you're going. You've known him for a while now, so don't give me that story about it being too soon to make your mind up!'

'I'll think about it. Thanks for being so helpful, Helen.' Patricia hesitated. 'And while we're on the subject of help, isn't it time you accepted more than that pittance we agreed on for looking after Emma? You're doing far more than we agreed on at the beginning and—'

'Shush! I only agreed to you paying me something because you insisted and I thought it would make you feel easier about the arrangement. But I adore Emma and she fits in so well with my lot that I miss her when she isn't here! Besides, what are sisters for…?'

As Patricia lay in the bath, surrounded by foam bubbles, she realised that her sister had been right about her relationship with Adam. It was all of ten months since she'd first met him and he'd made such an impact on her feelings. She wouldn't have thought it possible for a heavily pregnant woman to fall in love at first sight but she realised that was what had happened to her. And even though there'd been a gap of six months between their first meeting and starting work together, he'd rarely been out of her thoughts during that time.

She remembered how, during the first weeks of Emma's life when she'd been coping on her own in that horrible flat in Leeds, her thoughts had turned to the knight in shining armour who'd ridden on his imaginary white horse to save her from danger when she'd struggled to produce her baby. She'd remembered the touch of his fingers, the good humour he'd shown, how he'd held her spirits up near the end of labour when she'd desperately wanted to scream out.

And she'd been embarrassed as she'd remembered how she'd bitten his hand at one point in an effort to prevent herself from screaming. But he'd merely held tightly to her with the other hand and hadn't complained. He'd even told her she was being very brave!

Patricia turned on the tap and added some more hot water, hoping it wouldn't give out before she'd indulged herself to the full. Her tiny hot-water boiler wasn't used to coping with luxuriously proportioned baths like this one. She squirted in some more of the bath foam that Helen and Brian had bought her last Christmas and which she'd been saving for a special occasion.

Well, it was certainly going to be a special occasion tonight. She was going to look her best, relaxed and pampered and ready to enjoy herself to the full.

Someone was banging on the door knocker. Maybe they would go away…but maybe it was something important, like Helen calling to pick up some more clothes for Emma.

She groaned as she hauled herself out of the bath and wrapped herself in a towel. Going to the bedroom window, she opened the casement and leaned out.

It was Adam!

'You're early! I wasn't expecting you for another two hours.'

He gave her a sexy grin. 'I know, but I couldn't wait that long. Will you let me in or do you want the whole of Highdale to know what we're up to?'

Patricia laughed as she scampered on wet, bare feet down the stairs. 'What do you mean, what we're up to?' she asked in a deliberately provocative voice as she opened the door just wide enough for Adam to get through.

He pulled her towards him and folded her in his arms.

'Mind your suit! I'm very—'

His lips silenced her protests. She savoured his lips hungrily.

'This is what we're up to,' he murmured as he nuzzled his head into her neck, before scooping her up into his arms and carrying her up the stairs.

The towel unwrapped itself and slithered to the floor but she hardly noticed as she clung to him, leaving her old workaday self at the bottom of the stairs. She'd already turned into the woman he loved to tantalise. She could feel the deep passion igniting inside her. She was turning into hot liquid, urgently seeking fulfilment from the only man in the world who could quench her fire.

Gently, Adam laid her on the bed. Her legs felt weak as she anticipated the joys of their love-making. She watched him tearing off his clothes, not taking his eyes from hers. Patricia pulled his naked body against hers, her fingers trailing over the muscles she had come to love so much. She knew every sinew of this wonderful torso, every secret place that gave her so much pleasure.

His manhood, pressing against her, excited her more every time they came together. This time was no exception. She could feel herself longing for the moment when their bodies would fuse but trying desperately to hold back so that she could prolong the ecstasy.

When he entered her she cried out with joy. Fulfilment was only a few rhythmic movements away and she wanted to savour it as the precious gift they shared between them…

Lying back on the bed Patricia turned to look at Adam, entangled in the damp sheets. She reached out a hand and he opened his eyes.

'Was that why you called here so early?' she whispered.

He pulled her into his arms again. 'It's so long since we were completely alone. I thought it was time we found out what it's really like to be just a couple.'

Her heart began to thud. Was he trying to move their relationship on from being simply a wonderful affair?

'We've always got the girls to worry about,' he said gently. 'Or work, or—'

'Or the ex-wife?' she said coyly.

He slackened his hold on her. 'Ah, I wondered when you would start to complain about Lauren.'

'I'm not complaining,' she said quickly. 'I'm simply pointing out that she does spend an awful lot of time with you and I'm not sure you should let her rely on you so much financially.'

'She's going through a bad patch,' Adam said carefully. 'Tony is grossly over-extended financially, and he's refusing to give her any more money. She thinks he's on the verge of bankruptcy.'

'Well, she'll have to get a job like the rest of us.'

He raised himself on one arm and looked down at her questioningly. 'If I didn't know you better, and the idea wasn't so ludicrous, I would say you were jealous.'

She took a deep breath. 'The idea isn't as stupid as you think. Lauren is a very attractive woman and—'

'Patricia, darling, where's your sense of proportion? The woman means nothing to me. You're the only girl in my life, you and Rebecca and Emma and…' He broke off, laughing. 'Is there anyone else I've forgotten?'

'I hope not,' she said, with mock severity.

'I think we just had our first lovers' tiff,' he said. 'So, while we're clearing the air, I want to ask you about Ben.'

'Don't you start! I had enough with Helen preaching at me about contacting him again.'

'I think you should.' Adam's expression was deeply sincere as he held her away from him so that he could look into her eyes. 'You've got to lay the ghost once and for all. Sooner or later you're going to have to start explaining to Emma and she'll be sure to want to see her biological father.'

Patricia turned away and clutched the pillow. 'I thought this was supposed to be a time when we didn't think about our responsibilities.'

'It is. Forget about it…till later.'

He pulled her against him and they lay together in spoon fashion until the contact of their two bodies aroused their passion once more…

Patricia looked up at the smart façade of the Country House restaurant. It was generally accepted to be the in place to come for miles around here.

'Fiendishly expensive,' her sister had told her that morning as she'd waved her off to go and pamper herself in preparation.

Patricia wriggled her toes in the strappy sandals as she climbed out of Adam's car. The pampering afternoon had left her in a languid state when she felt every part of her body, both inside and out, had been relaxed to the point that she wanted to go on living in this cloud-cuckoo-land for ever.

Adam's fingers curled around hers as he helped her out. She stayed for a moment looking up at him, reminding herself that it was only this evening that mattered. The rest of their lives would fall into place as long as she didn't start worrying.

The sun was beginning to sink below the hills that formed a backdrop to this intriguingly different old building that was full of character. The date, carved above the door, was 1675.

'It used to be a gentleman's residence until the gentleman became too impoverished and had to sell it for commercial purposes,' Adam said, as he steered her through into the wide, oak-panelled hall. 'One of the big hotel chains has taken it over but they've been discreet enough to keep it looking as much like a private house as possible.'

They were shown to a corner table beside one of the mullioned windows that looked out over the rose-filled garden.

'Pity I'm driving, so I can't drink,' Adam said, looking down at the list of cocktails. 'But you can. What would you like?'

Patricia shook her head. 'I'll join you in something fruity like a Pussyfoot or something.'

'I've got a bottle of champagne in my fridge for when we get home,' he told her as the waiter went off to fetch their drinks. 'We can have a party... just the two of us for once.'

'Your place or mine?' she said lightly.

'Mine,' he said firmly. He was studying the menu.

'I'm going to have the seafood *panachée* to start with and…'

The waiter was placing their drinks in front of them with an exaggerated flourish and placing a tempting-looking plate of canapés in the middle of the white linen tablecloth. Patricia took a sip of her delicious fruit juice as she decided what she would order.

'And after the seafood,' Adam was saying, 'I'll have the confit of duck with truffled green beans.'

'The marinated fillets of mullet with avocado for me,' Patricia told the waiter, 'followed by the Normandy pheasant.'

The evening passed for Patricia in a dreamlike state of the senses. She floated along, trying a little of this, a tasting of that. The portions weren't too large and she was happy to enjoy the ambience in a state of hazy delight. Sated by the afternoon's sensual pleasures in Adam's arms, she simply wanted to be with him. She didn't need anything more to complete her happiness.

They chose to have their coffee served in the sumptuous drawing room.

Adam leaned back against the comfortable cushions of the large sofa. 'So, what are we going to do about Ben?' he asked gently.

At the sound of that odious name she felt as if a cloud had suddenly darkened her horizon.

'Adam, this is my problem, not yours.'

'Oh, no! It's very much my problem as well. Until you've resolved what you're going to do about him we can't—' He broke off, glancing sideways to follow her reaction.

'We can't what?' she asked, holding her breath.

'We can't move on to a fresh start… You and I can't pretend we exist in isolation… What I'm saying is that family is everything. My father missed out on seeing me grow up and—'

'But that was his own choice, just as Ben has chosen to forget about Emma and me.'

'Ben made that choice in the heat of the moment. You told me you had a row when he came to see you in Leeds. He's had time to think things over and he's probably regretting how he behaved, but maybe he's too proud to admit it.'

Adam hesitated, reaching for her hand to bring it to his lips and gently press a kiss against her palm.

'I told you my father left me a letter, didn't I?' he said quietly. 'It arrived with the news of his death. I carry it around in my pocket all the time.'

She watched, fascinated, as he pulled a thin sheet of paper out and handed it to her.

'Read that,' he said, his voice husky with emotion. 'This is the father who walked out on me.'

Patricia looked down at the shaky writing. There was no address, no date. She began to read it silently.

Dear Adam, They tell me I haven't got long to live. It was the booze got me in the end. The old liver is not as good as it should be or something. I hope they find you to tell you that I thought about you a lot after I left. I tried to find where you were a few years ago but it was so difficult. I gave up in the end. You might not have wanted to see me, anyway. You must be well grown up by now. Never was any good at dates. Never was much good at anything except I made a bit of money out here and I want you to have it.

Patricia raised a hand to brush away a tear that was threatening to fall before she continued reading.

I hope you've got a good job, but money isn't every-thing. If I had my time again I'd make sure I kept the family together. I've often wondered about you. It's a pity I never saw you growing up.

                                    Your loving Dad.

She handed back the paper, taking hold of Adam's hand to give him a comforting squeeze.

'That letter must be very precious to you. It must be comforting to know that your father never forgot you.' She hesitated. 'I'll contact Ben,' she said quietly. 'If he chooses to opt out that's his decision. I won't try to persuade him.'

He nodded. 'Just give him the chance to change his mind and—'

'Dr Drayton?'

A waiter was standing over her, holding a cordless phone. 'There's a call for you.'

Patricia's first thought was that something had hap-pened to Emma. She grabbed the phone but didn't at first recognise the distraught voice.

'The hospital says they've got a kidney that is a match for Craig but he's refusing to leave the house. The am-bulance is here and—'

'Is that Mrs Watson?' she broke in.

'Yes, it's me, dear. I rang your sister and she told me where you were. I'm that worried he'll miss his turn.'

'Why won't he go in the ambulance?'

'Says he's scared of the operation. He wants you to be there when they do it.'

She drew in her breath. 'I'll come over to the house at once and try to talk some sense into him.'

Adam was looking at her enquiringly as she cut the

connection. 'Drive me over to the Watsons' house,' she said tersely. 'I'll explain on the way.'

The two ambulancemen standing outside the Watson house were stamping their feet as the nocturnal cold bit through their summer uniforms.

'We've got a right one in there, Doctor,' one of them said, recognising Patricia from the many times she'd called into Moortown General. 'Time's knocking on and he won't get his operation if he doesn't stop playing silly...you know.'

'I'll have him out in a couple of minutes,' she said firmly. 'Trust me!'

'Trust me, I'm a doctor,' quipped the driver of the ambulance, settling into his seat and starting up the engine. 'Come on, then, let's see some action.'

Patricia knew she hadn't a moment to waste.

Craig was lying on his bed listlessly, a frightened expression in his eyes. He visibly brightened as Patricia and Adam went in to see him. Patricia went across to the bed and took hold of Craig's hand.

'Craig, we've got to go now. If we don't get to the hospital soon there's a strong possibility that they'll give the kidney to someone else.'

'I don't want to go unless you'll stay with me all the time—in the operating theatre and everything. I want you to promise to be there when I come round and—'

'I'll be there all the time,' she promised, remembering the friends and colleagues she had in the urology department. She was confident that she could persuade them to allow her in to observe the transplant operation.

She left the bedside for a few seconds to unhook Craig's dressing-gown from the bedroom door.

'Now, put this on, Craig, and let's get going.'

The young man hesitated briefly, but as Patricia held out the garment towards him he complied, his eyes on her face all the time.

'That's my boy!' she said in a soothing tone, and she tied the knot of his belt.

'I'm trembling so much I don't think I could have done that,' Craig said in a quavering voice. 'It's such a big step, isn't it?'

Adam leaned forward to put his arm around Craig's shoulders and help him off the bed. 'Yes, it is, but we've talked about it a lot, haven't we? And you've always said it was what you wanted. Now, don't worry. You'll get one of the best transplant teams in the world.'

'And I'll be with you all the way,' Patricia said gently.

Adam's arm was still around Craig's shoulder as he went slowly towards the door.

At the door, Craig turned to look at Patricia. 'Couldn't you ask them to let you put the kidney in for me?'

'I'm a GP, Craig,' she said quietly. 'You need an experienced surgeon to perform the operation. And, believe me, you'll get the best in the profession.'

Craig took a deep breath. 'OK, let's go.'

The bright lights over the table were dazzling as Patricia went into the theatre, suitably gowned and masked. Craig's motionless form lay on the table. There had been no problems when she'd asked a friend of hers if she could be allowed into Theatre as an observer and Brendan Smythe, the consultant urologist who'd been called in to do the operation, hadn't objected.

She watched as he made the first incision, before beginning to cut through the layers of tissue beneath the skin. He raised his eyes briefly as a member of the donor team came in with a container which held the precious kidney.

Patricia wondered briefly about the donor. Maybe it had been a road accident. She hadn't enquired as she'd waited whilst Craig had been prepared for Theatre. It was sad to think that someone had died, but at least it wouldn't have all been in vain. Craig was going to get a new lease of life.

Brendan Smythe was now removing the diseased kidneys. As he replaced them with the healthy kidney she thought how much simpler it looked since her medical training days. Things had moved on since then. Technique and equipment had improved considerably.

It seemed a very short time before the surgeon pronounced that the kidney was in place.

She breathed a sigh of relief. They weren't yet out of the woods but Craig was hopefully well on the way to making a good recovery.

'You need to get some sleep,' Adam said, as Patricia met up with him in the medical residents' sitting room. 'I've had a snooze while I've been waiting. Come on, I'm going to take you home. Do you need a coffee before we go?'

She shook her head. 'I just want to get to my bed.'

'Your own bed?' he asked.

Patricia gave him a wry smile. 'Afraid so. I could sleep for a week. We'd better postpone the champagne party.'

'I'll hold you to that,' he said tenderly.

'I was there when Craig came round from the anaesthetic so I was able to tell him the operation was a success,' she said, as they walked together down the cor ridor. 'I don't know how much he'll remember of what I said, but—'

'But you've done all you're going to do for a few hours,' Adam said firmly. 'I'll phone your sister when it's breakfast-time and ask her to keep Emma for the morning.'

'Thanks, Adam.' Patricia climbed into the passenger seat and leaned back against the cushions as he closed the door then went round to the driver's seat. She closed her eyes and was instantly asleep.

It was only as the car came to a halt outside her house that she wakened, confused by what was happening.

Then she remembered the whole scenario. First there had been Adam's early appearance, an afternoon spent making love, an evening devoted to good food and conversation. There was something that Adam had asked her to do. Whatever was it?

She remembered! 'I'll contact Ben,' she said quietly.

'But not now,' he said gently, as he kissed her tenderly on the lips. 'Unless he's on night duty he'll be fast asleep. Later today will be time enough.'

CHAPTER EIGHT

AFTER a chilly, wet August, the summer weather finally returned in September and the whole of Highdale was enjoying the sunshine. Looking out of her consulting-room window, Patricia could see a group of children sitting on the garden wall, kicking their heels as they waited for their young friend to emerge.

The little boy she'd just treated and handed over to Lucy had fallen off a wall down in the holiday village just like the one his friends were playing on now, and she suspected he'd fractured his left ulna. He'd told her he'd put out his hand to save himself and then he'd felt a lot of pain.

From the angle at which he was holding his arm, the swelling around the fingers and the obvious pain, she'd deduced there was a fractured bone in his arm and had given a quick call to the hospital to ask them to treat him. An X-ray would confirm her diagnosis and then he would require plaster.

Lucy had offered to drive him down to the hospital as the parents didn't have a car and the ambulance service were stretched to the limit during the mornings. The receptionist tapped on her door and came in with the required hospital forms for Patricia to sign. The little patient trailed in after her, sucking the thumb of his good hand.

'We're off now, Doctor. Danny's mum has gone back to the holiday chalet because she had to leave the baby with a neighbour. I don't mind taking Danny by myself.'

Patricia was busy signing forms. So much paperwork just to get an X-ray and a simple plaster! She broke off to stroke Danny's fair hair.

'You've been a good boy for me, Danny. You're a brave little soldier. Just keep it up for Lucy, won't you?'

Danny nodded, but continued sucking his thumb.

Patricia handed Lucy the paperwork. 'What would we do without you, Lucy?'

Lucy smiled as she put the forms in her bag, took hold of Danny's good hand, even though he objected to the removal of his thumb, and made for the door.

She turned round to look at Patricia. 'The place would fall down without me, I expect! Oh, I nearly forgot. You've got a visitor. Says he's called Dr Farraday.' She lowered her voice. 'I've no idea what he wants.'

Patricia's heart sank. 'I have,' she said tersely. 'You can send him in.'

Wasn't that just like Ben, to turn up at the end of a long working morning? It must be over a month since she'd sent him that letter asking him if he would like to come up to Yorkshire to see his daughter.

Lucy had left the door open. She swallowed hard as Ben appeared and stood, waiting to be invited inside. He was wearing one of his posh suits but he looked a bit crumpled and tired as if he'd had a long journey. And he hadn't even combed his usually immaculate fair hair. Was it her imagination or was his hair beginning to look a bit thin on top? It definitely had a few grey streaks which she hadn't noticed last time she'd seen him.

'Aren't you going to ask me in?'

'The door's open,' she said evenly, and then, remembering that she was supposed to be negotiating for a truce, she stood up and gave him a faint smile. 'Do come in, Ben. When did you arrive?'

He sat down in one of the patients' chairs. 'Just now. Thought I'd never find the place. All these winding roads! And mud everywhere! My car looks as if it's been in the Monte Carlo Rally.'

'Bit different to London, eh? Would you like a coffee?'

'Black, no sugar.'

'I remember.'

Patricia was glad of the excuse to leave her room to make the coffee. Lucy had already gone so she put the cafetière on the hob, trying to gather her thoughts.

She'd thought about what she was going to say so often since she'd written the letter, but now that he was actually here...

For one awful moment she thought the hands squeezing her shoulders were Ben's. She swung round and let out a sigh of relief as she saw who it really was.

'Adam, you gave me such a fright, creeping up on me like that!'

He kissed the tip of her nose and she leaned against him. 'I thought you were Ben.'

'Ben? Ah...the nice car outside. Dark blue Mercedes. I wondered who it belonged to as I came in just now off my rounds. Craig Watson's doing fine with his new kidney. His old girlfriend was with him, staying for the weekend apparently. Mother Watson doesn't entirely approve, of course, but she'll go along with anything that keeps Craig happy.'

Patricia smiled. 'I'm glad he's getting his life back together. Would you carry in this tray for me? I'm feeling so nervous I—'

He put one finger under her chin and tilted up her face so that she had to look straight into his eyes.

'I'm with you all the way on this, Patricia. Don'

worry. Once we've resolved what he wants to do about Emma, everything else will fall into place.'

He picked up the tray. She followed behind, taking deep breaths.

Adam put down the tray on her desk and held out his hand towards Ben.

'I'm Adam Young.'

'Ben Farraday. Do you work here?'

Adam nodded. 'I joined the practice at the same time as Patricia. We actually had our final interviews on the day that Emma was born.'

Patricia busied herself with the coffee. She handed a cup to Ben who was looking slightly puzzled.

'You mean you had your interviews together, but if Patricia was giving birth…'

Patricia gave a wry smile. 'I was actually in the first stage of labour when I came for the interview. Adam took me to the hospital when I'd finished the interview and stayed with me until Emma was born.'

'I see.'

Patricia noticed he was looking from one to the other of them. Only a blind man could have failed to see the rapport that existed between them, and Ben, she remembered, was very astute. He had to be in his work as a psychiatrist. When she'd been engaged to him she'd often felt he'd been analysing her behaviour.

'So, how is she—my daughter?' Ben fixed his eyes on Patricia.

Yes, those were definite grey streaks at the sides of his fair hair, she noticed. He was looking much older than his forty years. Was this due to the strain of being a consultant perhaps, or the worry of his personal life?

'She's fine. She'll be a year old next month.'

'She's just started walking,' Adam put in animatedly.

'Well, when I say walking, I mean hauling herself up and then staggering a few steps before she falls in a heap.'

Adam's proprietorial pride wasn't lost on Ben.

'You obviously see a lot of my daughter, Dr Young,' he said evenly. 'You and Patricia must be good friends by now.'

'Call me Adam, please. Yes, we spend a lot of time together. I have a daughter of my own. Rebecca's five. Her mother and I are divorced.'

'How...how convenient.'

'What's that supposed to mean?' Adam said sharply, dropping his initial effort to be polite.

'You get rid of one wife and plan to find another one to help you with your family life.'

'Now, just a minute,' Adam said, getting up from his chair and taking a step towards Ben.

'Gentlemen, let's keep our cool, shall we?' Patricia said quickly, putting a restraining hand on Adam's arm.

She turned to look at Ben. 'Yes, Adam and I are very close, but his marriage ended a long time before we met.'

'You didn't stay long enough with me for us to get married,' Ben said heatedly. 'I was planning to be completely faithful to you after we were married, but you didn't give me a chance, did you? Just flounced off without listening to my explanation.'

He banged his coffee-cup down on Patricia's desk, spilling some of the coffee onto some papers.

Patricia reached for a tissue, slowly mopping at the brown liquid as she tried to regain her calm.

'And what exactly was your explanation of the fact that you were sleeping with someone else?' she asked quietly,

'Catherine is an old friend,' Ben said, defensively. 'She'd just started work at the hospital as a junior doctor on my firm. I'd taken her out to dinner, had too much to drink…and one thing led to another.'

'But you'd cancelled your trip up to see me that weekend so you must have planned to—'

'Well, yes, I had planned to take Catherine out because…'

Adam sank back into his chair and clapped his hands together. 'Do you think we could stop the recriminations long enough to talk about the real issue?'

'Which is?' Ben faced Adam with a defiant expression.

Patricia cleared her throat as she prepared to spell it out as succinctly as possible. 'Do you want to see your daughter, Ben, and do you want to be involved in her upbringing, or would you simply like to go back to London and forget that—?'

'Well, of course I'd like to see my daughter!' Ben said loudly. 'We didn't get off to a very good start last time I came up here. And I'd like to see her now and again, but as for contributing towards her education and so forth…'

'This has got nothing to do with financial involvement,' Adam said evenly. 'Patricia is merely giving you the chance to take an interest in Emma's life if you want to.'

'The problem is…' Ben said carefully, as he looked from one to the other of them. 'You see, Catherine and I are planning to marry at the end of the month. She's already six months pregnant with twins, and with my new family to consider it would be financially draining to take on—'

'So the one-night stand developed into something important, did it?' Adam asked in a bland tone.

Ben looked down and started fiddling with his silk tie. 'As I told you, Catherine was an old friend. We'd had an affair…some time before I met Patricia. After Patricia walked out on me, Catherine and I simply carried on where we left off. We didn't plan this pregnancy, but when Catherine told me she was pregnant and wanted to get married, well…'

He looked up and stared defiantly at Adam.

'Anyway, I don't have to justify myself to you. All I'm saying is that I won't be able to contribute as much as—'

'I don't want your money, Ben,' Patricia said, trying to keep her voice calm. 'I pity poor Catherine if the only reason you're marrying her is because she's pregnant. That would never have happened in my case. I prefer my independence as a mother.'

'So you have no plans to marry again?' Ben asked.

'No plans at all,' she replied quietly.

Well, it was true, wasn't it? Even though she was in love with the most wonderful man in the world, she didn't know whether either of them were ready to commit to that ultimate step towards losing their independence. Adam prized his independence as much as she did, and she didn't want anything to spoil what they had between them by formalising their relationship.

'You always were a tough character,' Ben said evenly. He glanced at his watch. 'So, when can I see Emma? I've got to be back in London this evening for a meeting. My diary has been full for weeks. I had a couple of cancellations so I rescheduled the agenda for today so that I could drive up here. I checked with your receptionist that you would be here.'

Patricia frowned. 'I'm surprised Lucy didn't tell me you were coming. She's usually so efficient.'

'Ah, well.' He hesitated. 'I didn't actually give my name when I rang up. So she probably didn't think it was important to mention that someone had asked if you would be here.'

'Quite!' Adam said, barely disguising his dislike of Patricia's ex-fiancé. 'May I suggest we continue this discussion at my house? I'll provide something for lunch. If you'd like to follow me in your car, Ben, Patricia will come along when she's picked up Emma from her sister's.'

Driving up the hill towards Adam's house, Patricia was feeling relieved that Adam had taken charge of the situation. She found Ben such a pain! What she'd ever seen in the man she couldn't think! But, then, he had always been very good at turning on the charm when it suited him…and switching it right off when he'd had enough. She really pitied his future wife. How awful to be shackled to a devious character like Ben for the rest of her life!

In her rear-view mirror she could see that Emma, strapped into her car seat, was watching her. She fervently hoped that her daughter wouldn't develop any of Ben's characteristics in later life. But nobody was all bad. And a good upbringing would rectify any genetic weakness. She would make sure she set a good example towards Emma in the years to come.

She frowned as she pulled into Adam's drive. Lauren's distinctive silver sports car was parked by the front steps. Why on earth was that woman here again? Rebecca was supposed to be at school so she must have come to see Adam.

Lauren came out onto the front steps, Rebecca holding her hand. Behind them a couple of small toddlers vied for their mother's attention.

'Hi, Patricia! I had to bring Rebecca home. She was sick at school. They've got a new secretary who phoned me by mistake. I had to bring Rowan and Theo with me. Our nanny walked out on me last week so I'm a full-time mum at the moment. We can't stay long but Adam's invited me to lunch so…how are you?'

Carrying Emma up the front steps, Patricia replied that she was fine, absolutely fine!

The twins began fighting and Lauren let go of Rebecca's hand to try and calm them.

'How are you, Rebecca?' Patricia said, bending down to give the little girl a kiss on the cheek. 'All better now?'

Rebecca smiled. 'Yes. My tummy was funny but it's OK now. I cried 'cos I wanted to see Daddy. Who's that man in the house he's talking to?'

Adam appeared, hurrying out through the doorway. 'Patricia, come inside. Let me take Emma.'

'Daddy, who's that man?' Rebecca persisted.

'That's Emma's daddy,' Adam said evenly.

'You didn't tell me that,' Lauren said, her face showing her surprise at this unexpected piece of news. 'You just introduced him as Dr Benjamin Farraday. I thought he was a visiting medical colleague from London. It's so inconsiderate of you not to put me in the picture. I didn't know—'

'Come inside,' Adam said impatiently. 'Perhaps you'd like me to give you Ben's curriculum vitae, Lauren?'

Walking ahead towards the kitchen, Patricia smiled to herself as she heard Adam's sarcasm. Sometimes his patience with his ex-wife simply snapped, and she wasn't surprised. Lauren would have tried the patience of a saint.

'Here's Emma,' Adam said, carrying her over towards Ben, who was sitting by the kitchen window.

Ben stood up and held out his arms as if to take the child. Emma buried her face in Adam's shoulder and refused to look up.

'She's shy with strangers,' Lauren said, pushing her way forward, the twins still scrapping and squalling behind her. 'She'll get used to you if you give her time. She probably doesn't realise you're her father, does she, Dr Farraday? When did you last see her?'

'A few months ago,' Ben said defensively. 'The problem is that Patricia insists on being completely independent, so I've had very little contact with my daughter.'

'I don't think that's the problem at all,' Patricia said carefully, as she took Emma from Adam and put her down in the play-pen with her favourite cuddly toys. 'But we won't go into that now.'

She held out her hands towards the noisy twins and smiled. 'Would you like to look after baby Emma for me? She'd love to play with you.'

The boys went quiet but, taking hold of Patricia's hand, they climbed over into the play-pen and started playing with the cuddly animals.

'Lauren, could you set the kitchen table, please?' Adam said, as he stirred a large pan of soup on the Aga.

Lauren glanced down at her immaculately manicured nails. 'Sorry, Adam. My nails are barely dry and—'

'I'll do it,' Patricia said, moving swiftly to clear the kitchen top where Adam had been cutting open some large packets of ready-made carrot and coriander soup whose distinctive, gaudy packaging pronounced the product to be from the new supermarket on the edge of

Highdale village which had sprung up to service the holiday village.

'Thanks, Patricia,' Adam said, quietly, as he continued to stir the soup. 'Ben had to come with me when I made a detour to Tony's new supermarket because I realised I didn't have any soup in the house.'

She threw the empty packets in the waste bin under the sink and wiped the surface, before opening the cutlery drawer. 'So it's Tony's supermarket, is it? I wondered who owned it. He must own half of Highdale by now.'

'They're talking about my husband, Tony—Dr Farraday,' Lauren said, smiling sweetly at Ben.

Ben smiled back. 'Do call me Ben, and may I call you Lauren?'

Lauren simpered. 'Please, do!'

'Your husband must be a very rich man if he owns all this property,' Ben said in a conversational tone.

Lauren laughed. 'He'd like everybody to think so—everybody but me, that is. He's desperately overextended financially at the moment. His bank manager is getting tough with him and it's only a matter of time before…'

She stopped, realising that everybody in the room was now listening to her. 'Well, that's his problem. He's been so mean with me lately that I don't care if the sky falls in on him. I'm going to leave him soon, but that means I'll have to go back to work.'

Patricia looked up from setting the table. 'Does Tony know all this?'

Lauren hesitated, glancing over at her daughter to make sure she'd joined in the noisy game with Emma and the twins and wasn't listening in to the grown-up conversation.

'We're living separate lives already. I only hope his new girlfriend can cope with him when it comes to the crunch.'

'What kind of work do you do, Lauren?' Ben asked.

'I'm an accountant. I can't find an opening around here that pays a decent salary so I may have to move south again. I've got an interview in London next week.'

'Won't you find it hard being a single parent in London?' Ben asked. 'Especially with a small daughter and twin boys.'

Lauren glanced nervously at Adam. 'I haven't thought that far. Rebecca loves living with her father so it may be best for her to stay here. The boys get on well with their father so... I only want what's best for the children, of course...'

Adam made no comment as he poured the soup into a large earthenware tureen.

Patricia busied herself with persuading the children to leave their game and come to the table. All four clutched the cuddly toys they'd been playing with as they left the playpen which, under Rebecca's instructions, had been turned into a miniature zoo.

The table was set, the plates were warming, Emma was in her high chair, banging her spoon impatiently as she gnawed on a piece of dry bread. The twins were seated on either side of Rebecca. Patricia surveyed the scene. It looked like a setting from a happy family advert, except that the underlying tension between the adults was beginning to show.

Adam placed the soup tureen on the table. Patricia had already put out four dishes of soup to cool for the children. She tested the smallest one.

'Just right!' she pronounced, putting the bowl in front of Emma and giving her a spoon in each hand. She

glanced at Ben who'd elected to sit at the far end of the
table away from the children. 'Emma pretends she's
feeding herself but a lot of it gets lost on her tray. I
manage to spoon some of it in like this…'

Emma made loud smacking noises with her mouth
and licked at some soup that had fallen on to the back
of her chubby little hand. Glancing down the table at
Ben, Patricia could see he wasn't paying any attention
to what his daughter got up to. She wondered if he
would be the same with the twins his girlfriend was expecting! Maybe he would mellow after they arrived.
Well, at least she'd made the effort to get him involved
with Emma.

You could lead a horse to water but you couldn't
make him drink. From now on it was up to Ben whether
he contacted her or not. She was only doing this for
Emma's sake. Maybe when her daughter had grown out
of the messy baby stage her father would be more
pleased to see her. For a psychiatrist he was showing a
remarkable lack of interest in his own child's develop-
ment!

'What the hell does he want?' Lauren had rushed to
the window and was glaring through the open casement
at an approaching car. 'It's Tony!'

Adam tried unsuccessfully to conceal a groan. 'Does
Tony know you're here, Lauren?'

'Not unless he's phoned the school. He was out when
I left.'

Lauren turned away from the window and marched
with determined strides towards the hall.

Patricia continued to spoon soup into her daughter,
whilst listening to see what would happen between the
estranged husband and wife.

There was a squealing of tyres outside and then

Tony's loud voice in the hall. 'Where the hell have you been this morning? You weren't answering your mobile and then I knew what you were up to. I just knew you'd come over to see lover boy!'

'Adam is my ex-husband!' Lauren screamed. 'Don't you dare come storming over here as if you own me.'

'Well, you're still my wife, even though I know you're trying to get back together with Adam. Deny it, will you...?'

Tony's accusations died away as he walked through into the kitchen.

'Quite a party you're having,' he said, staring around the room. 'Hello, Adam. I expected you and Lauren would be in the bedroom by now.'

Patricia could see that Tony's eyes were bulging in their sockets. His normally florid face was now bright red and beads of sweat were standing out on his forehead. He was breathing in a rapid, stertorous way that worried her. He looked in a worse condition than the last time they'd seen him. He definitely wasn't well.

She glanced at Adam and saw that he was looking at her questioningly. As if by telepathy they both took on their professional personas and moved towards Tony. His wounding words meant nothing to Adam as he endeavoured to calm down the overwrought and obviously sick man.

Patricia waited beside Adam as he put a hand on Tony's shoulder.

'I can see you're upset, Tony, so why don't you come and sit down and—?'

'Upset!' Tony roared, banging his hand down on the kitchen table so hard that the cutlery and plates rattled.

All four children began to cry.

'Lauren, would you mind taking the children into the

garden?' Patricia said in as calm a voice as she could muster.

'Why don't you take them into the garden?' Lauren said angrily.

'Because I'm a doctor and I want to help your husband,' Patricia said evenly. 'I can see he's sick and requires medical attention.'

Ben suddenly sprang into action. 'I'll take care of the children,' he said firmly. 'This is far too stressful a situation for them.'

He was already hauling a protesting Emma from her high chair. Rebecca, who had gone very quiet, slid off her chair and escaped into the peaceful garden away from all the shouting. The twins followed her.

'There's nothing wrong with you that couldn't be cured if you didn't drink and eat so much!' Lauren shouted at her husband. 'Have you looked in the mirror lately at your gross, flabby body? How could you expect me not to prefer Adam to you?'

'There!' Tony wheezed triumphantly. 'I knew something was going on between you!'

He was fiddling inside his pocket. 'Can't find those damn tablets,' he muttered under his breath. He was clutching at his chest. 'I just need…'

Adam caught him as he fell. The huge man taxed all his strength but he managed to lower the man carefully to the floor without injuring him.

Lauren screamed. 'What's the matter with him?'

'Tony's having a heart attack,' Adam said tersely, leaning over the unconscious figure as he tried to find a pulse. 'Go into the garden, Lauren, and help Ben with the children. You'll only get in the way if you stay in here.'

'I can't find a pulse,' he told Patricia, ignoring Lauren

who was still staring down at the inert body of her husband.

'Is he dead?' Lauren whispered hoarsely. 'He doesn't look as if he's breathing at all.'

Adam glanced up at Lauren. 'We're going to try to revive him. Now, will you, please, leave us to get on with it?'

They worked together in tandem on the cardiac resuscitation, Adam exerting fifteen compressions to the chest for every two mouth to mouth breaths that Patricia gave to the seemingly lifeless figure.

On the tenth sequence, there was a slight movement of the chest and they suspended the treatment.

'He's coming round,' Patricia said, breathing a sigh of relief. 'There's a faint pulse here at the temple.'

She sat back on her heels and her eyes met Adam's.

'This was just waiting to happen,' he said quietly. 'Tony, can you hear me?'

'What…?' Tony mumbled, trying to sit up.

'Don't try to move, Tony,' Patricia said, holding the big man by the shoulders. 'You've had a heart attack and we're going to get you into hospital.'

She could hear Adam on the phone, making the arrangements. He was requesting an ambulance urgently.

'Let me put this cushion under your head like this,' she said quietly.

'I feel awful,' Tony moaned. 'Give me a drop of whisky, there's a darling.'

'Sorry, Tony,' Patricia said. 'They'll want to do some tests when they get you to hospital and—'

'Yes, but this is medicinal, isn't it?'

'Just keep still, Tony,' Adam said, kneeling down beside him. 'The ambulance will be here in a few minutes and—'

'Now I remember,' Tony said, his voice faint and hoarse. 'I came out to bring my two-timing wife home.'

'Tony, Lauren wasn't two-timing you...well, not with me anyway,' Adam said.

'Well, it was you she wanted,' Tony said, his voice barely audible. 'Always saying she was hoping to get you back.'

'No chance!' Adam said. 'But you shouldn't be worrying about anything at the moment. Just concentrate on resting or you'll work yourself up into another state and we might not be able to bring you round next time. You've been very lucky.'

'Thanks, Adam.' Tony closed his eyes and his breathing became slower and more shallow.

Patricia glanced anxiously at Adam. 'How long will the ambulance be?'

'They know it's urgent. We'll give him some oxygen as soon as they arrive.'

CHAPTER NINE

LAUREN rushed into the kitchen from the garden. 'There's an ambulance coming up the drive. I'd like to come to the hospital with Tony.'

'It would be better if you stayed to look after the children,' Adam said, going towards the front door.

'But I'm his wife!' Lauren declared petulantly. 'If anything happens to Tony…'

'That's OK,' Ben said, appearing at the kitchen door. 'You go along to the hospital, Lauren. I'll cancel my meeting and stay to look after the children.'

Patricia glanced at her ex-fiancé. Standing outside the doorway, with Rebecca on his shoulders, Emma on his hip and the twins clinging to his rumpled trouser legs, he looked like a good-natured family man who was used to coping with children all the time. She remembered that he'd actually studied child psychology. Maybe some of his formal training was coming in useful. Whatever it was, it made her remember, briefly, how much she'd cared for him when they'd first gone out together.

So she hadn't been such an idiot to have chosen Ben after all! Which was what she'd been thinking ever since he'd cheated on her.

As she'd told herself before, nobody was all bad. And it was so good to see him bonding with his daughter. He'd claimed that she was too independent and had kept him away from his daughter. That wasn't true, but she certainly hadn't encouraged him to see Emma. She'd felt a guilty pang about that. She'd wanted Emma to be her very own baby and nobody else's.

Listening to the ambulance pulling to a halt in front of the steps, Patricia found herself thinking that sometimes it took a tragedy like a heart attack to bring out the best in everybody. Looking at Lauren now, with the tears streaming down her face as she clutched Tony's hand, you would have thought she was the perfect, grieving wife.

'Through here,' Adam said, directing the paramedics who were carrying a stretcher.

Tony was loaded carefully into the ambulance. Adam fixed an oxygen mask over his mouth. Patricia sat beside him to monitor Tony's heartbeats which were unsteady and faint.

'I'm going to fix up a saline drip so he doesn't become dehydrated,' Patricia said. One of the paramedics passed her the equipment.

Lauren sat at the other side of the ambulance, biting her lip as she tried not to dissolve into tears again. After her initial outburst, Adam had asked her to try to keep quiet if she could.

Tony seemed unaware of his surroundings as the doctors and paramedics fought for his life. He was drifting in and out of consciousness. Arriving at the hospital, the cardiac team took over. Lauren insisted she wanted to go with her husband to Intensive Care but Patricia and Adam were told they didn't need to stay now that their patient was in good hands.

They took a taxi back to Highdale. As it drove up the drive, Patricia exclaimed in surprise at the sight that greeted them.

'Now I've seen everything!'

Ben was crawling around the grass, growling like a

bear, whilst Emma, Rebecca and the twins took it in turns to ride on his back.

As he stood up when they arrived, Patricia could see the grass stains on his otherwise immaculate trousers.

'How's the patient?' he called.

'He's in Intensive Care,' Adam said. 'I'm going to call back this evening for a progress report.'

Ben nodded gravely. 'I'm a psychiatrist, not a cardiologist, but you only had to look at Tony to see it was simply a matter of time before his heart started protesting.'

He looked down at his trousers and gave a wry grin as he brushed off some grass. 'My dry-cleaner will wonder what I've been up to on my trip to the Yorkshire Dales. I'd better start the drive back to London now. Penny, your part-time help, has arrived. She's inside, but the children wanted to stay out here with me.'

Patricia detected a note of pride in his voice. 'Can we get you something before you go, Ben? I can heat up the soup we didn't have time to finish at lunchtime or make a cup of tea.'

He shook his head. 'I didn't cancel my meeting. If I go now, I'll catch the end of it.'

Patricia and Adam waved him off as he drove away down the drive.

'Come up for Emma's birthday next month,' Patricia called.

'I'll have to look in the diary,' he called back. 'Be in touch.'

He was once more the uninvolved man who'd arrived earlier that day.

Penny came out of the house. 'Would the children like to have their tea now?' she said, holding out a couple of biscuits in front of her as an inducement.

Adam, who was holding Emma, handed her over to Penny. Rebecca held out her hand for a biscuit.

'Please, Penny!'

Patricia watched them disappear into the house before she turned to look at Adam.

'You know, Adam, the good thing that's come out of today is that I've been able to see Ben bonding with his daughter. As she grows up she won't have to wonder if her natural father loves her, because I think he really will. I'm glad you insisted I make the effort to contact him again. I didn't want to. I was happy having Emma all to myself, but you've always got to think of how the child will feel in later years. They need to keep in contact with both their natural parents if it's at all possible, don't they?'

Adam put an arm round her shoulders. 'And the events of the day also made a few things clearer to me which have been puzzling me. Like some of the ideas that Lauren has hinted at, especially over the last few weeks when she hasn't had any money and I've been helping her out. One mad idea was that the two of us should take Rebecca away on holiday together. She said it would be good for her. Of course, I knocked that one on the head as soon as she brought it up. The idea of spending more than a few hours with Lauren fills me with horror!'

Patricia looked up at him. 'Surely you weren't in any doubt as to what she was up to, were you? I certainly wasn't!'

He pulled a wry face. 'I think women are more perceptive about these things than men. I was merely making sure that the mother of my daughter was able to look after her without worrying about money. But all the time—'

He broke off and then smiled as he remembered something amusing. 'She was always talking about the good times we'd had together, and I thought it was strange that she was being so nostalgic. Lauren hasn't got a sentimental bone in her body.'

'Didn't she make any more obvious suggestions about getting back together again other than going away on holiday?'

He frowned as he thought hard before shaking his head slowly. 'But last week she told me she'd dumped the new boyfriend she had because she wanted to make herself free for a more permanent relationship.'

'And you never suspected what she was up to?'

'Maybe I suspected she was up to something,' he said, 'but the idea of Lauren and me being together again is too ludicrous to contemplate. Now that I've found out what real love is all about...'

His eyes were, oh, so tender as he gathered her into his arms. 'My feelings for you are light years away from anything I ever experienced with Lauren all those years ago.'

She swallowed the lump in her throat. 'It's the same with how I felt about Ben and how I feel about you, Adam.'

'I love you, Patricia,' he said, his voice husky with emotion.

She could feel her heart pounding so loudly she was sure he could hear. 'I love you, Adam,' she whispered.

He bent his head and kissed her, gently at first and then with a fierce passion that threatened to sweep them both off to some quiet place where they could consummate their love.

Adam pulled himself away and looked down at her, his breathing rapid. 'Will you marry me, Patricia?'

She held her breath. This question from the man she now loved more than her own life had sometimes been part of her dreams. It was one of the fantasies that had kept her going when it had seemed totally unlikely that it would ever materialise. But now here she was, with the man of her dreams, and it was all actually happening.

'I would like to be with you for the rest of my life,' she began, carefully choosing her words because her whole future depended on what she said now. 'But...' She hesitated, wondering how she was going to explain her fears about the future.

'So what's the problem?' His eyes were searching her face, trying to understand her less than enthusiastic response.

'The problem is that I love the relationship we already have together. I love being with you and yet keeping my independence. I worry that marriage with all its conventional trappings might change us into—'

'Darling, nothing will change. Married or not married, we'll still love each other in the same way. OK, if you're worried about marriage, we'll simply live together. No strings attached. You could move in here with Emma who would grow up with Rebecca. You and I would continue our wonderful romance together. Nothing would change between us. And maybe...just maybe...'

She waited as she watched Adam struggling to put his thoughts into words.

'Maybe we could have a baby of our own. There would be yours, mine and ours...but only if you were happy with the idea. It's just a dream at the moment, but...'

'Yours, mine and ours,' she repeated quietly. 'I like your dream— in fact, I love it.'

He kissed her gently on the lips, his arms caressing her gently.

Patricia looked up into his dark, expressive eyes. 'It's all happening so quickly. I just need a little more time before I can give you an answer...'

She broke off, glancing at her watch. 'Shouldn't you be going off to do evening surgery?'

He smiled. 'When I phoned Richard and Jane from the hospital to let them know we'd been treating a cardiac patient, Richard told me not to come in this evening. He said he would do the evening surgery.'

'So we've got a free evening,' Patricia said, feeling the happiness welling up inside her.

Adam grinned. 'Can't think what we'll do when all the children are in bed. We'll have to keep Rowan and Theo here, of course, because Lauren will be staying at the hospital with Tony. They can sleep in the bed in Rebecca's room. Let's go in and make an early start on the bathing. We'll send Penny home and I'll cook supper for us as we missed our lunch. After that...'

They carried the remains of the wine up to the bathroom to drink while they had a long soak together. Patricia wiggled her toes around Adam's neck.

'Sorry you drew the short straw and got the end with the taps,' she said, luxuriating back against the bath cushion.

He flipped some foam towards her. 'I always draw the short straw. I'm planning to install a huge bath for when we get...when you come to live here.'

'I like the sound of that. It's not desperately comfortable at this end either. But I enjoy the feel of your skin on mine.'

She snuggled lower down the bath. He leaned forward

and kissed her before turning her around so that they were lying spoon-shaped along the length of the bath.

'Mmm, that's better,' she whispered as she stretched out her legs against his. She could feel his aroused manhood pressed against her and her own passion grew inside her. Patricia closed her eyes to savour the blissful feelings that were running like electric currents over her entire body.

As if in a dream, she felt his arms lifting her out bodily, wrapping her in a warm, scented, fluffy towel, carrying her into the bedroom.

They made love hurriedly, each of them anxious to slake the passion that their togetherness always brought on. And then, taking their time, they tantalised, savoured, explored and brought each other to climax after climax until a delicious ethereal sleep claimed them, sweeping them off to a dream world where the real world didn't exist…

Patricia woke in the middle of the night, pulling up the sheet as a light breeze blew in through the open casement. To her surprise, Adam was awake, leaning up on his arm, looking down at her with a puzzled look on his face.

'What's the matter?' she whispered.

'Nothing's the matter,' he said huskily. 'Everything's just perfect, so why can't you make up your mind?'

'I will make up my mind,' she said gently. 'Just give me time.'

'Emma's first birthday,' he said decisively. 'You can have until Emma's first birthday in six weeks' time.'

She smiled. 'And that's an ultimatum, is it?'

'Absolutely! After that…'

'After that, you'll offer the situation of wife to one of your other girlfriends, will you?'

'Something like that.'

Adam leaned forward and kissed her tenderly. 'I didn't use a condom tonight.'

'I did notice,' she whispered. 'Was that in preparation for our own little one?'

'We had discussed it, hadn't we? The possibility of extending our family?'

Patricia nodded happily. 'Yours, mine and ours.'

He drew her closer. 'But they'll all be ours really. There'll be no difference in the way we care for them, will there?'

'Of course not. They'll be our little nest of babies wrapped round with as much love as we can give them.'

'I'm glad we agree on something,' he murmured as he pulled her even closer against his hard, muscular body, his hands beginning once more to caress her in the way that drove her wild with desire.

'I think we agree on all the important things,' Patricia whispered, giving herself up to the fresh longing that was mounting inside her.

'Emma's birthday. That's the ultimatum,' he said, his voice husky with desire. 'You'll have known me for ages then so you can't possibly think you're on the rebound from Ben. And you've had lots of time to get over his devious ways, so you can't use that as an excuse to procrastinate...'

His lips on hers made it impossible to reply, even if she'd thought out her answer—which she hadn't. But she would have to in the next six weeks.

Why was it that she had this fear of commitment when she loved Adam so much and wanted his children? What was she afraid of?

CHAPTER TEN

IN THE end everybody helped Emma to blow out the candle on her birthday cake. She had giggled and laughed when it had been placed on the tray of her high chair, stretching out her plump little hands towards it, but she had refused to follow Patricia's miming motions about blowing.

All the children had left their seats at the kitchen table and gathered round to help.

'Shall we blow out your candle now, Emma?' Rebecca said, assuming the role of big sister as she always did when they were together.

Emma continued to laugh. It was such fun to be the centre of attention! Such fun to have a bright burning candle in front of her!

'Come on, everybody!' Rebecca said as she blew hard at the large, solitary candle on top of the pink and white gooey cake Patricia had made.

Patricia left Rebecca to get on with it while she made sure that Rowan and Theo didn't push the high chair over as they surged forward noisily.

Lauren, in a designer suit, was standing well back from all the sticky fingers. As Patricia took the cake away to the worktop at the side of the kitchen in preparation for cutting, she handed the two-year-old twins into her sister Helen's care.

'Gemma will help me with these two little boys, won't you?' Helen said to her daughter. 'They're the same age as your brother Tom.'

Gemma, who'd just had her fifth birthday, beamed with delight at being elevated to little mother as she found toys for all three small boys to play with.

Jane, who'd just arrived from doing an afternoon clinic at Highdale Practice, put sixteen-month Edward with the other boys and sat down on the floor to help entertain them.

Adam picked up the large knife and began to cut the cake into small child-size pieces.

'Lovely cake, darling,' he said, removing a squiggle of icing from the top so that the knife would go in straight.

Patricia laughed. 'I've never made a cake before...as you probably guessed from the mess I had to clear up at the end of it! I followed the recipe exactly but I don't think it should be quite so gooey.'

'The kids won't notice. So long as it sticks to their fingers and gets in their hair...'

'Have you got a cloth I could mop the floor with?' Helen said. 'Rowan's just spilled his juice.'

Patricia went over to the cupboard under the sink. She glanced out of the window at an approaching vehicle as she handed over the cloth to her sister. It was almost like a rerun of the lunch party six weeks ago as she recognised Tony's car coming up the drive. Oh, no! she hoped he wasn't here to create trouble.

As she swung round she noticed that Lauren had already noticed Tony's arrival.

'Were you expecting Tony to come, Lauren?' she asked anxiously.

Lauren smiled. 'We're only running one car now. Part of the new economies we're having to make. Tony dropped me off earlier and said he'd come back for me.'

'I didn't notice,' Patricia said.

'You were busy making sandwiches when I arrived,' Lauren said. 'Tony didn't want to come in for the party. Not his scene.'

Patricia was intrigued by the new ambience of togetherness. Lauren's voice was altogether softer when she spoke about her husband. Could it be Tony's heart attack and the thought that he could have died which had brought about this transformation? Lauren had certainly seemed to ditch all her plans about leaving him.

'See if you can persuade him in for a piece of cake, Lauren.'

Lauren laughed. 'He doesn't eat cake any more—it's not on his diet sheet. But I'll see if he'll come in for a minute or two. I'd like you to see how good he looks since he went on a healthy eating plan and gave up the booze.'

As Tony came into the crowded kitchen, Patricia had to stifle a gasp of astonishment.

'A shadow of your former self,' Adam said, as he came forward to shake the new slim-line Tony by the hand.

Jane got up from the floor, carrying her son with her, and went to join them. 'I can see you're sticking to the health plan I gave you.'

Patricia joined the admiring group standing around Tony. 'You're in better shape than you were the last time you came here.'

'I haven't had a chance to thank you and Adam,' Tony said in an uncharacteristically subdued tone. 'I owe my life to you. When I came out of hospital, the specialist had fixed an appointment for me at the Highdale Practice.'

'It just so happened that I was on duty that morning,'

Jane said. 'And Tony's stuck with me ever since and been one of my most determined patients.'

'I remember you telling me that I wouldn't live to see my twins' next birthday if I didn't change my eating and drinking habits, Dr Jane,' Tony said sombrely. 'So I didn't have any option, did I?'

He was surveying the scene in the kitchen. 'Where's that nice chap who was here last time I came? The day I nearly died. He was so helpful with our boys. I wanted to thank him for looking after them so that Lauren could come to the hospital. She told me afterwards that he was Emma's father.'

'Ben sent his apologies but he couldn't get up here for Emma's party,' Patricia said quietly. 'He sent her a beautiful doll and he's promised to be here for her second birthday.'

Patricia wiped the last plastic mug and put it away in the cupboard. Helen had insisted on mopping the kitchen floor before she'd left, but there had been so many footprints over it since then that it looked pretty awful again.

'I'll just give this floor a quick swipe with the mop and then—'

'Oh, no, you won't,' Adam said, taking the mop from her hand and placing it against the wall. 'We have far more important things to do with our time.'

He drew her into his embrace and she leaned against him, glad of the support as she gave in to the feeling of weariness that had suddenly hit her at the end of a long, busy day.

'It was a good party, wasn't it?' she said. 'Wonderful to see Tony looking so well. Do you think he and Lauren are getting back together again?'

'Who can say? I think they both had a major shock

when he nearly died and it brought them to their senses. They probably realised that they still love each other.'

'It often takes a near tragedy to bring people to their senses.'

'What will it take to bring you to your senses?' he asked quietly.

She pretended she didn't know what he was talking about. 'I don't follow you.'

He smiled. 'Don't play games with me, Patricia. You know what day it is.'

'Emma's birthday. This time last year I was in the throes of labour.'

'And we'd only just met. But, as I keep reminding you, we've become much closer since then. So, have you got an answer to my all-important question?'

She looked up into his eyes, her heart brimming over with love as she hugged her secret to herself.

'I've made up my mind,' she said. 'This morning when I woke up, I could see our wonderful future together, stretching ahead into eternity, and I knew, like you said, that a love like ours is a once-in-a-lifetime experience. Nothing in the world can compare with what we've got between us. And then later, when I stared at that thin coloured line, I—'

He looked down at her with a perplexed expression. 'What thin coloured line?'

'Remember we talked about yours, mine and ours? Well, yesterday I got a pregnancy testing kit and this morning I used it.'

'Darling!'

He was squeezing her so hard she could hardly breathe.

'When I stared at that thin line I knew this was the icing on the cake. I love you so much, Adam. I think always have, ever since that first day when you were so wonderful with me. And my love has grown more and more over the time that I've known you. Nothing can change that love. We'll be parents together but deep down we'll still be the same lovers that we are now, with the added joy of yours, mine and ours. So if you were to ask me again…'

'You mean you want the whole works? Down on one knee and all that?'

She laughed. 'If we're to be married we're not going to do it by halves. All or nothing!'

He was pretending to complain as he went down on one knee but when he raised his eyes to hers she felt herself drowning in his loving, tender expression.

'Will you marry me, Patricia?' he said, his voice husky with emotion.

'Yes. Oh, yes…' That was all she could manage before he swept her up in his arms again and carried her to their bedroom.

'We need to sort out the prenuptial agreement,' he whispered as he laid her lovingly on their four-poster bed. 'Important things like how many children we're going to have and—'

'You mean after this one?'

'It might be twins…'

'Would you mind if it was?'

He kissed her slowly, savouring the feel of her lips against his. 'On second thoughts, let's postpone the discussion for a little while…'

MILLS & BOON®

Makes any time special™

Mills & Boon publish 29 new titles every month. Select from...

Modern Romance™   Tender Romance™

Sensual Romance™

Medical Romance™   Historical Romance™

MAT2

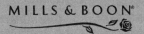

Medical Romance™

EMOTIONAL RESCUE *by Alison Roberts*

Newly qualified ambulance officer Hannah Duncan
soon realises that she loves her job – and her
colleague Adam Lewis! But he doesn't want children,
and Hannah already has a toddler of her own. Will
she be able to help rescue Adam from the demons of
his past and give them all a future?

THE SURGEON'S DILEMMA *by Laura MacDonald*

Catherine Slade knew she was deeply attracted to her
boss, the charismatic senior consultant Paul
Grantham. She also knew he had a secret sorrow
that she could help him with. If only a relationship
between them wasn't so forbidden…

A FULL RECOVERY *by Gill Sanderson*

Book two of Nursing Sisters duo

If he is to persuade emotionally bruised theatre nurse
Jo to love again, neurologist Ben Franklin must give
her tenderness and patience. But when she does
eventually give herself to him, how can he be sure
she's not just on the rebound?

On sale 3rd August 2001

*Available at most branches of WH Smith, Tesco,
Martins, Borders, Easons, Sainsbury, Woolworth
and most good paperback bookshops* 0701/03a

A Perfect Family

An enthralling family saga by bestselling author

PENNY JORDAN

Published 20th July

*Available at branches of WH Smith, Tesco,
Martins, RS McCall, Forbuoys, Borders, Easons,
Sainsbury, Woolworth and most good paperback bookshops*

4 FREE

books and a surprise gift!

We would like to take this opportunity to thank you for reading this Mills & Boon® book by offering you the chance to take FOUR more specially selected titles from the Medical Romance™ series absolutely FREE! We're also making this offer to introduce you to the benefits of the Reader Service™—

> ★ FREE home delivery
> ★ FREE gifts and competitions
> ★ FREE monthly Newsletter
> ★ Exclusive Reader Service discounts
> ★ Books available before they're in the shops

Accepting these FREE books and gift places you under no obligation to buy, you may cancel at any time, even after receiving your free shipment. Simply complete your details below and return the entire page to the address below. *You don't even need a stamp!*

YES! Please send me 4 free Medical Romance books and a surprise gift. I understand that unless you hear from me, I will receive 6 superb new titles every month for just £2.49 each, postage and packing free. I am under no obligation to purchase any books and may cancel my subscription at any time. The free books and gift will be mine to keep in any case.

M1ZEA

Ms/Mrs/Miss/Mr ....Initials....................................
                                                         BLOCK CAPITALS PLEASE

Surname ....

Address ....

....

....Postcode..............................

Send this whole page to:
UK: FREEPOST CN81, Croydon, CR9 3WZ
EIRE: PO Box 4546, Kilcock, County Kildare (stamp required)

Offer valid in UK and Eire only and not available to current Reader Service subscribers to this series. We reserve the right to refuse an application and applicants must be aged 18 years or over. Only one application per household. Terms and prices subject to change without notice. Offer expires 31st January 2002. As a result of this application, you may receive offers from other carefully selected companies. If you would prefer not to share in this opportunity please write to The Data Manager at the address above.

Mills & Boon® is a registered trademark owned by Harlequin Mills & Boon Limited.
Medical Romance™ is being used as a trademark.